PRAISE FOR THE WORKS OF
TIMOTHY W. LONG

"If this is how the world ends, sign me up!"--
Jonathan Maberry, *New York Times Best Selling
author of Patient Zero*

"One of the best zombie novels of the year."-- *Paul
"Goat" Allen, Barnes and Noble*

"Long, a prolific horror author writes with graphic
glee - repulsive details and way off-color jokes
abound. If this were a movie, it would be rated R
for revolting but it's revolting in a cheerful kind of
way."-- *Tacoma News Tribune*

Also by Timothy W. Long

Beyond the Barriers (Permuted Press)
Among the Living (Permuted Press)
Among the Dead (Permuted Press)
Among the Dead (Coming Soon)
At the Behest of the Dead
The Zombie Wilson Diaries
The Apocalypse and Satan's Glory Hole
Z-Risen: Outcasts (Coming Soon)

Credits:
Edited by T. F. Rose
Cover art: Straight 8 Custom Photography
Interior art: Zach McCain

TIMOTHY W. LONG'S

In the event this log is found with my corpse, I'm Machinist Mate First Class Jackson Creed and it's been a week since we arrived back in San Diego following the event. With me is Marine Sergeant Joel "Cruze" Kelly.

We were both stationed on the USS McClusky, an Oliver Hazard Perry-class frigate out of San Diego. Our ship was overrun by the dead and we barely escaped with our lives. Now we live in the middle of Undead Central.

###

BEER RUN

The fuckening has become more bearable even though we almost joined the crawlers today.

Supplies:

- A pound and a half of Jasmine rice
- A half pound of dried beans
- Two pounds of that tofu-jerky shit that gives me gas
- Seven cans of tuna
- Two cans of cat food that I'm saving for Butch in case he returns
- A case of canned spinach that I eat even though every bite makes me want to puke my guts up

I want to go on record as saying that this whole stupid day was Joel's fault.

###

18:25 hours approximate.
Location: Undead Central, San Diego, CA

"Look at all of those crawlers. Everyone wants a piece of us," Joel whispered. "Must be my good looks."

I snorted.

Joel was dressed in tactical gear with a New York Fire Department ball cap pulled down low to keep the sun off his face. Beneath the hat, he wore a pair of Tom Cruise-style Ray-Bans we'd found in an overturned car.

Joel was prone and staring down the barrel of his Rock River Arms AR-15. He switched on the EOTech holographic sight and shifted his aim left and right.

We'd found the assault rifle the day after we founded Fortress, not far from our area of operations. Some civilian had purchased the piece and stored it for a rainy day, or the end of the world. Yeah, I see the irony. It was so new that it still had the manual and price tag. Even the magazines hadn't been unpacked. The second bonus had been a green canister filled with 400 rounds of 5.56.

Joel was probably sweating his ass off in all that gear. The one thing he managed to escape the ship with was most of an IMTV - Improved Modular Tactical Vest.

"Let's make sure they don't get a piece. I like all my limbs," I whispered. "How many are there?"

"Six, and there's one of those weird shufflers."

I popped up and did a quick scan. Five of them were moving around the freaky creeper. The shuffler was down on all fours like a retarded crab missing a few legs. The other Z's were your garden-variety dead. They moaned and cast milky white gazes on nothing in particular while they shambled.

We were perched behind an abandoned house about a mile from the naval base. Our area of operations had spread out over the last weeks as we ranged farther and farther away from the fortress. It had to be done; our search for food and supplies was getting harder every day.

This had been a residential neighborhood with an elementary school and apartments along a large main road that led to Interstate 5. There were a number of houses, but most had already been ransacked. Some sported graffiti and broken windows. Most had furniture and belongings dragged out onto front yards and dumped next to corpses that, thank God, did not move.

We'd learned the hard way not to bother with the houses. Walk in an open door and it could become a deathtrap. Open a bedroom and it could be filled with the fucking Z's. When panic hits and you're in an unfamiliar location, suddenly you don't know which way to exit.

"Your call. I'm good and didn't need a beer run in the first place," I lied.

I needed a beer run bad. I'd kill for a cold one but would settle for a six-pack of warm. But this mission was more than about getting a few brews. If his friend was still alive we might find food and a more secure location to call home.

My gut rumbled, thanks to our light breakfast of dried tofu and some leftover beans and rice. God, what if he had potato chips and Little Debbie Cakes? What if Kelly's friend had boxes of crackers and Cheez Whiz? My mouth flooded with saliva and I feared the creepers would hear my stomach rumble. This wasn't just about beer. We needed anything we could scavenge.

It was getting close to dusk. A bead of sweat formed on my shaved head and ran down my forehead. I wiped it with the ridiculous orange sweatband around my wrist. Joel had been sick of me bitching and dug it out of an overturned bin in a Walmart we'd raided a few days ago. The rest of the store had been a bust. By the time we arrived, it'd been picked over ten times. We also found out the hard way that it was filled with about a hundred snarling Z's. When we got out, I wore the sweatband to remind myself to never enter a big department store again.

"Go distract them. See that dumpster at three o'clock? Just poke your head around it and say hi. I'll pop a couple in the head. When they come toward the sound of my shots, you finish off the rest with your club." He nodded toward my wrench.

I shaded my eyes and studied the battlefield. A green dumpster sat next to a low wall. There was a break right next to it that would provide me with an easy way to get on the party's "six." I bet Joel thought it was funny as hell, sending me out with my ass exposed while he shot from a distance.

"I don't like it."

"Roger that. Let's pack up and go home."

"Well, hold up there a second, Professor," I said. We might not have a chance to explore this area again. "If we leave now, your friend's place will be picked over. Might already be empty."

"I told you. He's a security nut. His front door is solid metal, plus he'd have left it bolted."

"I still don't know how we're going to get in."

"If he's not there, I have a plan." Joel didn't turn but he had that cocksure sound in his voice that I no longer questioned.

"What if he is there and tells us to fuck off?"

"He won't. He owes me." I didn't ask about Joel's time in Iraq because it pissed him off.

After a few seconds of cursing, I hefted my wrench. At twenty-four inches and eight pounds, this was a devastating weapon when applied to Z's heads. Joel chambered a round but didn't look back to make sure I'd left. After a week of this shit, we were like goddamn mind readers.

"Stupid fucking idea," I said under my breath, and moved around a dying hedge.

I dropped low and hoped there weren't another dozen hiding behind us. You could lose them if you moved fast or stuck to shoot-and-scoot tactics, but try to make a stand and it was a quick trip to Undeadville.

I rounded the block and cut back toward Joel's position, sticking to a sidewalk that was already overgrown with grass. I constantly scanned my surroundings, looking for the slightest hint of additional Z's.

The red wrench wasn't my only weapon. I also wore one of the newer Colt M45A1 pistols on my hip that I'd taken from a corpse back on the base. I had one extra mag and a pocketful of rounds in case things got real hairy. What concerned me was the noise a booming gun could draw. I might as well attract a horde with all six-feet, three-inches of me bouncing up and down while singing the national anthem.

The thirty or so rounds did make me feel better. As long as I kept an extra one in the little coin pocket at my right hip, I felt like I was safe. I'd take as many of them as I could, but that last bullet had my name on it.

Literally.

Sun glistened on my arm to reveal that I was still losing muscle mass. I needed protein, not beer, but I'd settle for a buzz after the last shitty weeks I thought back to the day when our ship, filled with undead sailors, plowed into the pier. Joel and I had been tearing through the passageways, firing into the mass that had previously lived on the USS McClusky.

I ducked again as one of the creepers looked my way. Milky eyes brushed over my position as I hit the ground. Even at a mere twenty feet away, I still marveled at their ability to actually see or hear a damn thing. As the days rolled by and they rotted a little more, they had to slow down and lose some of their senses. At least, that was my logic. It's one of those things you tell yourself over and over. It's not that bad, it's not so crazy out there. Things will get better in a few days, just wait it out. But that didn't happen.

One thing that did grow was their hunger and, as that got stronger, so did their need to eat. Us.

I used to read zombie books and think Z's would be about as scary as drunken senior citizens. These weren't. They had started mad and gotten madder. The shufflers were the worst. When they changed, so did their disposition. Not content to wander around mindlessly, they were driven by a need to rise and attack, and they'd go psychotic whenever they spotted the living.

The slow ones weren't so bad, but get twenty or thirty of those relentless fucking monsters on your case, and they'd run you right into the ground.

I scanned my entry point and crouched again, then brushed past another dying hedge. I rounded the corner near the dumpster and the pack came into view.

I slid next to the giant green monstrosity and plugged my nose with my fingertips. Foul, very foul. I stood and waved a hand in the air, hoping to hell Joel wasn't currently getting swarmed. Then I stopped. What use was it? He wasn't about to announce his hiding place.

"You ugly godless fucks come here often?" I lowered the wrench, letting all 8.4 pounds of the weapon become an extension of my arm.

The creeper that had fixed his milky gaze on me earlier turned his head on his creaking neck and drew back desiccated lips over rotted teeth. The others swiveled to take me in. A chill raced over my body at the thought of one of those assholes sinking their teeth into me.

One shot and the creeper's head popped to the side, followed by his body. Brain matter splattered and blood sprayed. Two Z's moved toward the noise, leaving three for me. Terrific.

"Hey assholes," called Joel.

I risked a glance at my watch. The action had already occupied five seconds of the thirty we allotted any battle. If we couldn't wrap things up in that time frame, we'd bug out.

I swung the wrench up and took the nearest right under the chin. I hit him so hard I thought his head was going to come off. Poor kid. Couldn't have been more than fifteen when he turned. Dressed in shorts and a gaudy t-shirt, he wore only one knee pad. He did have pads on both elbows, though. Probably some skate punk that was now a dead punk.

The second Z closed in. I gave ground, lifted my size fourteen US Navy-issued boot, and kicked him in the groin. That didn't put him down but it bought me a moment. As far as I knew, they didn't have functioning nads, but a swift kick could still put them in their place.

Another pair of shots, but I had things to worry about other than Joel's body-count.

I didn't have time to beat these things to death, so I drew the M45 with my left hand, aimed just as I'd practiced a hundred times over the last couple of weeks, and shot one through the neck. It sounds cool but I was actually aiming for its forehead. I'd lowered the gun just a fraction at the last second.

The Z fell away, gurgling blood from its neck. I aimed and fired at the shuffler but it was already on the move. It'd been caressing the ground on all fours, doing that shuffle step that freaks me the fuck out. The man had long wisps of hair hanging from his scalp and, somehow, a pair of glasses perched on the remains of his face. His mouth was full of blood, drool, and something that looked a lot like human flesh.

I fired again. The bullet punched through his gut just before he smashed into me.

I hit the dumpster hard enough to knock my breath out and staggered to the side. He fell away but was on his feet in a flash. His eyes had the same milky white look but they somehow fixed on me. He howled a wordless scream of fury and launched himself. I swung the pipe but there wasn't a lot of strength behind it. The glancing blow barely kept him from biting my arm.

I staggered back again and bullets whizzed through the air, taking the creepers out with extreme prejudice.

I fired again, but the shot went wide because I'd panicked. The shuffler didn't cower, it didn't hide, and it didn't turn and run. It was completely unreasonable—and its only desire was to rip into my flesh.

I gave ground, fighting for breath, and when he attacked again, I punched him. I didn't get a lot behind the strike but it was enough to knock the Z down. I lifted the gun, took a half breath, and blew his fucking brains all over the pavement.

Joel moved in on my position, Ray-Bans looking everywhere as he ran. He had the assault rifle across his chest, finger on the trigger guard. We didn't stop to admire our handiwork. Instead, we moved out at a fast clip because we were well over our thirty seconds and that was bad news. Another half minute and we'd be overrun.

###

18:45 hours approximate
Location: San Diego, CA

We exited the block and ran into the parking lot of an apartment complex. Joel and I had dodged behind cars and concrete dividers at every opportunity. Our sprint had carried us nearly a hundred and fifty yards away from the dumpster and I, for one, had begun to feel it.

I panted, hunched next to a car; Joel did the same. He swept his ball cap off his black head and wiped sweat from his brow with his sleeve. San Diego might be a comfortable seventy degrees but running for your life has a tendency to make you sweat like a pig.

I pointed at my orange wristband and he gave me the finger. While we took a breather, I ejected the magazine from the M45 and filled the five rounds I'd emptied into Z's. Joel took a moment to do the same with his AR. We waited and looked toward the area we'd just left, only to find that luck was on our side and we'd avoided a larger confrontation.

I eyed car interiors while Joel stayed on point. I actually found an old beat-up Ford that hadn't been broken into and pressed the end of the wrench against the closed window. I looked around quickly, then pulled back and hit it just hard enough to break glass. It imploded with a soft pop and tinkle. I opened the door and felt around under the seat and came up with a small paper bag. The glove box had some mints and papers. I slid the items over my shoulder and into my Swiss Army backpack as I moved out.

"What's in the bag?" Joel whispered.

"Not sure. It's not very heavy; check it when we're clear?"

"Sounds good." He moved out in a semi-crouch, rifle stock pressed to his cheek.

We advanced on the apartment complex and came to a cross-street that had been a battlefield. Police cars overturned next to military vehicles. Blood splatters everywhere. Broken bodies, both civilian and military, lay on the pavement or over car hoods. Some hung out of broken windows, faces torn away or necks gnawed to the bone.

"Fuck me," Joel said, and moved to a body. We did a quick check but only came up with a few stray rounds. Someone had stripped this place clean.

Joel eyed a map and then we were on the move again. A few minutes later, we had the condo in sight.

No Z's in the immediate vicinity. Luck was on our side, for a change.

We dashed across what was once a very expensive plot of grass but was now a dry and yellowed bed of tinder. If a stray spark caught, this whole block would go up in flames.

We reached the stairway without challenge. At the top of the second flight, Joel advanced down a hallway on the outside of the building while I followed. Doors had already been ripped open and goods tossed on the balcony. Joel didn't bother with the residences and kept moving with me right behind.

"This is it," Joel said.

We'd reached something different, a solid door with no marks around the door jamb. Someone had tossed a car jack to the ground in frustration.

Joel knocked gently.

"Ty. You there, Ty? It's Joel Kelly from the base. Come on buddy, at least let me know you're on the other side of that door."

He knocked a few more times then shook his head in frustration.

"What's the plan?"

"Watch my back."

Joel glanced left and right, dropped the backpack, and went to one knee. He rummaged around in the bag until he came up with a MacGyver-looking complement of tools and wires. He'd split a large coffee can in half and lined the concave surface with grey packs of something that looked dangerous. He yanked out a double wrapped freezer bag of water and added it to the package.

"The fuck?" I whispered.

Joel shook his head and held the can up against the door. He broke out duct tape and applied a few strips until the device was held in place. He stood back and tugged a wire out of the side of the can, then looked around again.

"Shit."

"What?"

"Be right back."

He dashed to the condo next to us and came out twenty seconds later dragging a mattress. I moved to help but he pointed at his eyes then forked his fingers, indicating that I needed to stay sharp.

Joel tugged the mattress over and draped it against the door. He pulled the wire out of the can while shielding himself with the mattress, then ran it down the hallway, gesturing for me to follow. We crouched around the corner while he plugged the wire into a detonator.

"Holy fuck balls," I whispered. "Don't. It'll wake up the whole city."

"In and out, buddy. In and out." Joel smiled, then held the device up.

"Dude. How many will that bring?" But it was too late. He already had his finger on the trigger.

I covered my ears; he tried to do the same by using one hand and an elbow. Even with the mattress in place, the explosion was immense. The building shook and dust and debris showered the floor. Joel was level-headed and didn't rattle easily, but when it came to fuck ups, this was a big one.

I looked at my watch and marked the time. Thirty seconds were going to come to an end very quickly. In fact, I doubted we even had fifteen seconds. Shaking my head, I followed him into his friend's condo.

I waved smoke out of my face as we entered. Joel had his assault rifle at the ready, so I followed suit and pulled out my M45.

The door had been blown off its hinges. Joel walked over it in a half-crouch. He had the AR level with his shoulder and aimed into the smoky interior. I followed closely but kept my eyes on the entrance. Just as I cleared the entryway I got a look over the railing.

I gasped and reached for Joel to get his attention but he wasn't there.

Out on the brown grass, the dead were gathering. Not a few, not even a dozen. It seemed like they were coming out of their undead comas from every corner of the city.

I swore and walked into the haze left by the explosion.

The entryway was a mess. The door had been blown into the small space and smashed whatever furniture had been there. The smell of smoke and explosives burned my nose. There was a mirror on one wall but it had been shattered, and when I looked into it, I saw my face splintered into five pieces.

"Ty, don't shoot us, man!" Joel called. "It's me, Joel. I told you I'd come."

Hey Ty, we just broke into your house but it's cool because you and Joel go way back, so don't, you know, blow us away. If someone broke into my castle I'd be pissed whether I knew them or not, and would probably shoot them out of pure spite.

"Joel!" I whispered as loud as I dared. "A shitload of dead are on the way. We don't have thirty seconds."

Joel came back into the hallway and gestured. I followed him into the living room and found it filled with tech gadgets. A huge flat-screen TV sat dead on the wall, surrounded by speakers and stereo equipment. There were cables and wires everywhere, some attached to a huge car battery. Whatever the occupant had been trying to do had gone to the grave with him.

In front of a gorgeous tan leather couch lay an unmoving figure. He was a black guy in his twenties, as far as I could tell. He couldn't have been dead all that long because his face wasn't a rotted mess. He had a series of bite marks on his arm, the same arm that held a handgun which had been applied to his forehead before a bullet had torn his brains out of the other side of his head.

"Goddamn," I said.

Joel dropped to one knee and said a prayer. He took the handgun from his dead friend's grip, hit the safety, and slipped it into the band of one of his tactical vest's many straps. He touched his friend's eyes below the bullet hole and tried to close them, but they were frozen open.

"I wish you would have held out, buddy."

I pointed out the bite marks. Joel stood up and moved away.

Joel and I advanced on the kitchen like the starving heroes we were. I raided the fridge and found Nirvana. A couple of six-packs of cheap PBR. An unopened package of store-bought pepperoni. No power, but that was okay. The fridge wasn't that hot and pepperoni could sit for days. Joel and I devoured a half-pound of the thin slices like it was fucking filet mignon.

"We. Need. To. Go!" I said as I swallowed.

He tore open cabinets while I inspected the pantry. Ty had left a lot of goods. There were boxes and bags of pasta, jars of sauces, and canned fruits and vegetables. I practically fainted at the bounty. The problem was that we couldn't carry all of it. I had my backpack and Joel had his, but if we weighed ourselves down, we'd be moving targets.

I grabbed the pasta and a few cans of fruit and jammed them into my backpack. I added one precious jar of spaghetti sauce and then tested the weight. I added a few cans of veggies, saw spinach and avoided it like the plague.

Joel moved beside me and packed his backpack as well. We'd been inside for a few minutes, and with every beat of my palpitating heart, I knew the dead fucks were getting closer.

"You pack the heavy stuff," he said, and handed me his backpack. "We're going out there and you're not letting go of my shoulder. We move as one until we're free of the mess."

"Why do I have to be the fucking pack mule?"

"Because you're built like one and I need to shoot shit."

He made all kinds of sense but I didn't have to be happy about it. Before we headed out, I grabbed a six-pack, jammed it into my backpack and tried to close the bag, but the beer stuck out of the top.

"Drop your wrench and use your Colt. It's going to get hairy."

"The fuck you say. I ain't leaving my weapon."

Joel wanted to argue - he gets like that - but we didn't have time. I jammed the tool into my belt and fought to keep my overalls straight as it tugged them down toward my knees. I shrugged and pointed at the door.

# # #

19:05 hours approximate
Location: San Diego, CA

We hit the landing and tore to the right. I gripped Joel's shoulder while he moved (once again) in a crouch. I drew my M45 and switched it to my dominant right hand. On the grass, an army of the dead had congregated. Joel leaned over the railing, aimed...and fired at a car of all things. What the hell? He'd picked a high-end BMW; when the bullets punched into the hood, they set off an alarm.

"Jesus fucking Christ!" I cried.

The dead turned toward the sound and I realized Joel was smarter than he looked. Give a Marine a gun and they suddenly turn into a fucking brain surgeon.

"Let's go."

We rounded the corner we'd hidden behind when Joel had blown the door off. I wished we could have stayed, but this place was going to be swarmed. Once the dead moved on, scavengers would surely pick the place over before we could make another trip. Dammit! The condo had been a treasure trove of goods.

We moved to the other side of the building and took the stairs. I'd been sweating before, but now the last few minutes of activity hit me. I was carrying about forty pounds on my back and we were rushing down hallways and stairs.

Luck was still on our side when we hit the ground level – it wasn't swarming with Z's. The car alarm continued to howl behind us, but that just drew away any that were on the other side of the building.

A small pack wandered away at nine o'clock. Joel motioned to stop and stay still. The pack didn't see us, so we moved toward the street. Making our way north, we skirted the block that hosted the swarm and kept on jogging. The pack beat at my back with each step and I had no doubt the wrench would leave bruises.

We came to a house and stopped for a breath. As I stood there gasping, Joel, with no respect for my lack of stamina, moved on. We rounded a corner, found a trampoline, a pool, and four Z's. I broke right and fired as soon as I had a bead. Joel followed suit and pumped two rounds into the lead crawler's head. The old man fell down but another, even older guy in a tropical-print shirt stumbled over him. Joel put that one down, as well, while I took out their wives. It must have been the world's worst pool party even before the shit had hit the fan. One of the women had to be in her sixties and was dressed in a one-piece swimsuit. I shot her out of pity.

We had to skirt a tall chain-link fence before the area started to look familiar.

Joel and I moved at a fast pace, again taking out stragglers as quickly as we could. A few more minutes of hiding behind houses, ducking behind cars, and then Fortress came into view.

The house we occupied was set behind a few tall trees. We'd boarded up everything on the first floor and had left no easy way to the second. We had a ladder, but it was buried under a pile of old leaves and branches, and when we were inside, we just pulled the ladder up. Even if Z's surrounded us, we'd be able to wait them out.

I still worried about determined human scavengers.

Joel moved out on point and I was left behind a hedge to catch my breath. I wiped sweat off my head again and studied the area. No zombies stumbling around made me smile. It had been a bitch of a mission but at least we'd made it with food and a six-pack of beer intact.

Then my day went downhill.

The first crawler broke free from a cluster of dying hedges and was followed by six or seven other equally ugly, rotting souls. White eyes swiveled to find me, and like an army, they advanced.

"Oh fuck-knuckle!" I swore, falling back and drawing my M45A1 as I went. I drew a bead, fired, and missed the head zombie—a guy dressed in a sanitation outfit. It was on me before I could scream for help and, just like that, I was fighting for my life.

I slammed it to the side, my forearm working like a hammer, but it just kept on coming. A shot rang out and I swore again. One thing we tried to avoid at all cost was the sound of gunfire near our home base. We'd already broken that rule twice in the last fifteen seconds.

Another shot and one of the Z's dropped. I punched my attacker again. His head cocked to the side, but then he snarled and I got a look at broken teeth. There wasn't time to make a smart-ass quip. I tried to avoid a bite but screamed in horror as his mouth closed on my arm.

Thank god for my jumpsuit. It was hot as hell but the zombie's mouth closed on fabric, and when he tore, he got a piece of that instead of my skin. I pushed him away, raised my Colt .45 and blew off the back of his head.

A shuffler took notice and was in the air before I could take aim. I emptied the magazine but didn't have a chance to reach for a fresh one because the shuffler came in with flailing arms and a screaming mouth. I kicked his legs out from under him and shrugged out of my backpacks so I could maneuver. When the shuffler hit the ground, I ducked away from his wild grasping, got behind him, and kicked him in the ass.

He went down but was back on his feet in a heartbeat.

I reached down and grabbed my wrench. When he leapt at me again, his mouth a snarling howl of hate, I swung the wrench around and caught his jaw, ripping it loose.

But that was the problem with shufflers. They were so psychotic that even a massive amount of damage couldn't put them down. Headshot or enough damage to squish the brain had to be applied.

Joel's AR jammed. He dropped it and drew the pistol his friend had used to kill himself, then moved on the last couple of Z's. He put one down and fired a few more times until the gun was dry.

The shuffler, minus a jaw and part of his face, was on me again. I stepped on the body of the sanitation worker I'd shot and went down on my ass. The shuffler, arms still flailing, hit me hard enough to knock the breath out of my body for the second time.

I got a foot up and caught him in the chest as he bent down for me. Joel barreled into the shuffler, allowing me to roll to the side. I came up slowly because my body was all beat to hell. Another Z was on Joel, so he drew his Ontario 498 combat knife and slashed the creature across the gut, spilling intestines in a wet pile of gore. He reversed his grip and drove the blade into the dead woman's head.

He faded back as the shuffler looked between us.

He must have made up his mind because he went for Joel, the remnants of his mouth producing gurgles in place of a howl of fury.

I grabbed the wrench and closed in on the shuffler. Joel saw me coming and pushed the psychotic Z back. I hefted my weapon and let him have it, crushing his skull like it was a soft egg. The corpse dropped to the ground; Joel nodded at me and then the wrench with a half grin.

We dragged the corpses away from Fortress, retrieved the ladder, and scurried up as soon as we were sure no one was watching. Inside, we unpacked our treasure. I was not a happy camper to learn that a couple of our beer cans had exploded in one of my falls. At least we survived another expedition and came back with food and a new weapon.

"Sorry about your friend," I said.

Joel nodded. "Thanks, man. We saw some action in Iraq. He always had my back and I had his. Like you and me."

"Are you going to look that sad when it's my turn to bite it?"

"Depends on if I have to put you down myself, motherfucker." He grinned.

I grinned back and we toasted the day with warm PBRs.

"Oh yeah, what was in the paper bag?"

I dug out the bag I'd pulled from under the front seat of the old Ford pickup and looked inside.

"Shit yeah," I said, and pulled out an ounce of weed with a California medical dispensary logo on the bag.

"Stay sharp and don't smoke that shit. You white boys get all sad-eyed when you're high."

"Only on special occasions. Besides, I bet we can trade it if we run into other survivors."

"Good call. I'm gonna go use a few baby wipes to take a bath." Joel rose to his feet and headed toward his room. "Good work out there, Creed. And thanks for saving my ass."

Joel nodded again and left.

I sat back and drained my beer, then eyed the weed. Special occasion, eh? How about still being alive.

This is Machinist Mate First Class Jackson Creed and I am still alive.

THE BOAT

10:35 hours approximate
Location: San Diego, CA – Fortress

Nothing to do except hang out and try not to kill each other. We're flush with supplies for a day or two but no reason to start stroking each other's egos after yesterday's mess. Frankly, I'm surprised we're still alive. And with all of these supplies I'm really missing Tylenol. My body feels like I worked out until I puked.

So the day we boarded up the place, Joel had the bright idea to fill the tubs with water. We drank until our eyeballs were floating and then we drank some more. Joel kept telling me what it would be like in a week when the water stopped running and he was right. Now the water tastes foul and I'm worried about mosquitoes. I run a vegetable strainer over the surface every few hours. Tomorrow I'll use cheesecloth but that won't kill parasites. So do we burn through the few remaining Sterno cans boiling water or just put up with a bad case of the shits?

Joel said we can treat the water with a little bleach but I'll be damned if I can find a bottle in the house. I guess we'll have to find some on our next run.

#

Supplies:

- 1 pound of Jasmine rice
- ¼ pound of dried beans
- 1 ½ pounds of tofu-jerky
- 7 cans of tuna
- 2 cans of cat food - where the hell is Butch?
- 6 boxes of pasta
- 1 beautiful jar of spaghetti sauce
- 5 cans of various veggies
- 2 cans of mixed
- 1 case of canned spinach

"When you gonna talk about how we met?" Joel pointed at my logbook. I had the pen ready to start recounting our day – and that was going to be boring.

Day X: Sat on ass. Stared at empty beer bottles. Pissed in a bucket.

"Like the day you bought me flowers and a drink?" I looked across the Sterno flame and batted my eyelashes at Joel. "Fucking Marines. Always trying to get into a lady's panties."

We had a can of water boiling up some rice so we could put it aside and let the grain set. It was the quickest way to accomplish two tasks. Boil water and have a little food in an hour. I'd probably toss in some tofu jerky just to add to the blandness.

Fortress was hot. It might be October out there, but this house hadn't had a breath of fresh air in days. No fans, no central air. That meant we sat in a room and fanned ourselves with a collection of Playboys I'd found stashed under a kid's bed.

"Yours were pretty fucking frigid," Joel chuckled, "and it took a whole bottle, but just like a Navy puke, you put out on the first date."

I stifled laughter.

"Too bad you couldn't get it up. You know they make little blue pills for that?"

Joel had his assault rifle stripped and was quizzing me on parts while rubbing them down with motor oil. His towel had been white a few days ago. Now it looked as grimy as gopher guts.

"Marines are giant blue pills. Just being in the Corps gets me hard," he said. "That's what my old Drill Sergeant used to say just before he quarter-decked the shit out of us."

"Drill Sergeants are like that. Dicks."

"He was just doin' his job. Gunny made me the man I am today."

"Hooah!" I said.

"They only say that in movies," Joel retorted.

"Imagine I'm Brad Pitt when I say it."

Joel held out a long piece of metal that looked like a tube. "What's this called?"

"The bolt thing."

He sighed and tossed it to me. "It's not called 'the bolt thing,' it's called a bolt carrier assembly and even Brad Pitt would know, because I bet he pays more attention than you whether he's stripping a gun or that hot wife of his. Now take this part." Joel gave me the charging handle, something I actually remembered the name of. I took the pieces and slid the handle into the bolt carrier assembly, locking it in place before giving it back.

"There."

"You ain't as useless as I thought."

"Guess not."

"Too fucking hot for this. Go write about the ship," Joel grumbled.

I'd avoided writing that chapter for a lot of reasons, but after the last few days of scrambling for survival I knew it was time to get it out of my system. If I waited much longer I was going to start forgetting important facts.

"Not yet. Man, I really want to say it."

"Don't. We made it and I don't need thanks. We wouldn't be here if we weren't a team, even if you are a stupid fucking hole snipe."

"Words hurt, Joel. Words hurt." I leaned over my friend. Even seated I towered over him, but he didn't back down.

"Why all that writing anyway? Never heard of a hole snipe fond of jotting things down besides readings."

"I always wanted to be a writer. Sue me."

"What-the-fuck-ever. Just do it. Write about the boat; we ain't getting any younger and we might be dead and eaten tomorrow."

"Ship, it's called a ship. A boat has oars - and what a morbid fuck you are today!"

"Like I said. What-the-fuck-ever. Just write it."

So I did.

# # #

05:45 hours approximate
Location: USS McClusky, San Diego CA

I had the worst fucking hangover of my life the day the world went to shit. I lay in my bunk, hand over my eyes, and dreaded going on watch. My head pounded and my mouth felt like someone shit in it. We ain't supposed to drink at sea but I'm a classic Navy alcoholic and I keep a stash of booze you wouldn't believe. Last night I dumped a third of a 2-liter Pepsi down the drain and topped it off with some Thai whiskey I picked up in Pattaya Beach.

That was only two hours ago. I barely got enough sleep as it was. Emergency flight ops had blown me out of my bunk, and that shit went on until dawn.

There were rumors that something big was happening back at base, and that's why we were recalled. Then flight ops had started and never ended. Helos arrived and departed every fifteen minutes – that should have been my first clue that something was really wrong.

I had about fifteen minutes to shit, shower, and shave. Smitty got to be an angry little bitch when I was late even though he'd never been on time for watch a day in his life.

Then the alarm sounded and I thought my head was literally going to explode.

"General quarters, general quarters, all hands man your battlesta..."

The first line wasn't even finished, unless you counted the screaming. I sprang up and jumped out of my top bunk. Why a top bunk after this many years in the Navy? Because I fucking like it, that's why.

I stared up at the speakers and wondered whose idea of a joke that had been.

"The fuck was that shit?" Feely asked.

He wore a pair of South Park boxers and socks that smelled like death. Feely had a weird OCD thing with socks and only changed them once a week. One time I bought him a bag of socks at the ship commissary and left them on his bunk. Gratis. He tossed them in the trash.

I dug out a pair of dark blue overalls and gave them the sniff test. Yeah, they'd get me through one more day. They weren't as bad as Feely's socks. Those fuckers were probably going to get up and walk around on their own.

Wanglund fell out of his bunk and looked ready to punch anyone that got in his way. His mustache was turning into a biker's handlebar, but with shore in sight today he'd be shaving it. CHENG might put up with that shit on deployment but not when we were headed for port. The thing about Wanglund was that he was bigger than me and I'm a big dude. He was a boiler tech and looked like a gorilla, with hairy arms and enough fur on his back to let him fill in for the next Planet of the Apes movie.

Wanglund also owed me a hundred bucks from our last game of spades. I'd mention it later when it wasn't so early in the morning and he didn't look like punching someone.

###

I trudged toward the engine room, already dreading the heat and noise. The ship hummed around me. That's the kind of environment you live in when you are stationed on a Naval vessel. It's never quiet, not ever. From the grind of machinery to the sound of forced air in nearly every compartment, all you get is noise. Then there are the smells: the oil, the fuel, the cleaning chemicals. It's an assault when you first board ship, but then you get back on land and suddenly you forget how to walk straight because the ground is no longer rocking and rolling under your feet.

I moved along the same bulkheads I'd passed every day for the last twelve months. Boring, white, yellow emergency lights in every corner. I didn't see any other crewmen and that was weird. Maybe everyone was up early for mess. Was there an inspection I'd forgotten about?

Earplugs inserted, I descended a pair of ladders and stopped for a cup of shitty coffee before heading to main control. The whine of the turbines would be deafening without earplugs. As it was, the tone was slightly less annoying that having a tooth drilled. The engine was insulated and taller than a greyhound bus. I glanced at a couple of dials. Everything nominal.

The Chief Engineer was sitting at the console while newly-minted Chief Harmikle stood watch over the room. I was surprised he didn't have his nose up CHENG's ass. I tossed him a quick salute but he didn't bother responding. Petty Officer Mahan had the helm. He was spinning the giant steam valve to slow the ship. It looked like we'd just come down from Flank 1.

"How long we been at Flank?" I asked him.

"Too long if you ask me. Some crazy stuff is going on back home, man. You're my relief, right?"

"Nah, I got Smitty."

"Damn, he's ill too. They took him to sick bay an hour ago."

"What happened?"

"No clue, man. I've been stuck here all damn night."

"Say again?" CHENG barked into the phone. Then he banged it on the desk a few times. "Say again! Don't make me come the fuck up there!"

"S'going on?" I asked Chief Harmikle.

"Some fucking bullshit on the bridge. Sent Keen up to take a look."

"Does he even know where the bridge is, Sir?" Keen was so new he hadn't washed the creases out of his BDU's.

"Doubt it." The Chief Engineer said, hanging up the phone and hitting me with that "officer look" that's supposed to intimidate. I towered over him by a good seven inches and had arms the size of his neck, but somehow he always made me feel like he could take me in a fight. Maybe because he never wilted or looked away from one of my "pissed off" looks that sent other guys scurrying.

"You go look for Keen, Creed," he ordered.

I almost smiled. Just a few minutes on watch and I was already on my first errand. Looked like some coffee in mess would be my first stop.

"And Creed, don't get lost up there."

I nodded, took my pounding head out of main, and started back the way I'd come. Well, fuck me six ways from Sunday. This watch was off to a shitty start, but at least I was out of the hot engine room.

I headed starboard hoping I'd run into Keen's skinny ass. Instead, I ran into a riot.

Something was happening, something big. The passageways on a ship are already small and when a bunch of screaming guys are occupying the one ahead of you it's not like you can find a way around. I'd have to walk back until I could cut across the center of the ship.

I assessed my options. Walk all the way back on a mission to find Keen? Nah. I decided I'd rather get into some trouble. My last Captain's Mast was six months ago.

Fuck it. I was due.

I passed berths and came to a cross-section filled with a riotous crowd. I hung back but didn't see any engineers to rescue and couldn't figure out who to hit first. Getting into a fight wasn't the best cure for a hangover but I'd settle for it today.

I didn't personally know most of these guys but they were still familiar. You spend a few months at sea with a hundred and seventy-five or so guys and pretty soon you know a lot of names. They looked like electricians with their pressed shirts.

"Can someone let me through before I start breaking stuff?" I bellowed.

That got attention, but the wrong kind. A Lieutenant with fresh bars turned on me and looked at my stenciled name.

"Creed. Get some security here, now. And don't yell on my ship again. Got it, Sailor?"

"Yes Sir," I muttered, wanting to punch his fucking lights out. Then I saw blood on his hands.

"Sir?"

"It's…I don't know. One of the radio techs bit one of my men and then both of them went nuts. Go wake up the Marines."

That was all I needed. Crazy-ass nerds biting each other? That wasn't my problem. I was going to continue my search for Keen but then remembered that the LT knew my name. He also knew my size and it'd take about three seconds to find me.

I knew where the Marines bunked but never ventured down there. Why should I? They never came to my side of the ship.

I huffed it down their ladder and found myself in near-darkness. It was still the middle of the damn night, so that made sense, but a couple of black guys in tank tops were throwing cards at a table. One of the men jumped up on his chair and threw the little Joker.

"Suck it!" He yelled.

I cleared my throat. "Sorry to interrupt, fellas, but some LT sent me. Some guys are biting each other and the LT wants security."

"See my shirt?" asked little Joker. "Do you see 'babysitter' stenciled on it?"

I looked. I squinted. I peered.

"Huh. Nope. Umm…what's your name, man? I need to know for the LT; you know how it is."

"GENERAL QUARTERS, GENERAL QUARTERS, ALL HANDS MAN YOUR BATTLESTATIONS. GENERAL QUARTERS…"

The voice trailed off this time without screams, but screams or not I was really starting to get a very bad feeling about today.

"Thought it was a joke before." The Marine nodded toward the speaker in the ceiling.

"That sounded legit," one of the other guys said.

They looked at each other and then back toward their bunks.

Then I heard a sound I'd never heard on a ship before. Gunfire.

The Marines went into some turbo mode, moving around each other like they had a secret language. Before I could scratch my balls more than once, the black guy that had given me a ration of shit was back and half-dressed. He buttoned up a shirt and stared at me like I was a stranger. His stenciled name read 'Kelly.' He wore an oversized vest of some sort and slapped it over his body, securing straps and Velcro here and there as he patted down pouches and pockets.

"Weapons locker!" One of the other Marines yelled and suddenly there were guns everywhere. Kelly strapped a belt around his waist with a holster and pistol. My fists were the only weapon I'd ever been even halfway shitty with.

"Secure yourself, Sailor! Stay or go - just keep out of our way."

"Fine man, whatever. Just don't shoot anyone by mistake. Especially me." I rattled off the coordinates I'd marked in my head when I'd left the LT. As soon as the men were assembled, Kelly nodded. He pulled his sidearm and racked the bolt back, did an inspection, and let it slam home. He slid it back into his holster and then was up the stairs as fast as Spiderman.

I followed them and hit the passageway while they moved out. I wasn't more than a few steps from the ladder when a guy screamed and bore down on me. I knew his name but not much else. Bauman was a skinny little guy that wore his pants too high on his hips. He was covered in blood from a wound on his skull. The blood streamed down his head and into another wound on his face. Christ! Most of his cheek was ripped away! He howled, creating a weird hissing sound.

"The fuck?"

"Move!" one of the Marines ordered.

I ignored him and stood my ground. Come on Bauman, if you got the guts.

In a heartbeat, the bloodied, howling sailor was on me. I lashed my arm out and punched him square in the middle of the face. His nose erupted around my knuckles and he went down like a bag of potatoes.

My hand hurt like a bitch but I wore my poker face for the Marines. See? I can be a badass too.

"Dude!" One of the Marines brushed past me and leaned over to check on the sailor I'd decked. I wiped blood on my pants.

"Hey man, he attacked me," I said.

Skinny Bauman should have been out for the day after the punch I'd landed, but his eyes snapped open as he howled and leapt up, landing on his knees with a crack of bone.

He spun and attacked the Marine. The sailor bit in and yanked flesh from the other man's arm until blood flowed. The guy screamed in pain, pulled his gun, and hit Bauman hard enough to knock out teeth.

"What the shit!" I backed up in horror.

Kelly moved to my side and watched with his mouth wide open as the Marine dropped to the ground and thrashed his body up and down. It looked like he was having an epileptic fit. My Aunt used to get those and they were not pretty. The downed Marine screamed, but then something quickly changed as his wails of pain became those of rage.

Bauman should have been completely knocked the fuck out - or even dead - but he staggered to his feet and raised his hands, which were twisted and splayed like tight little claws. He howled again, that awful hissing sound now bubbling with blood, and then he was on us.

Me and Kelly beat the shit out of the guy, but every time he went down he just got back on his feet and came at us. Then Kelly's marine buddy went bat shit insane.

What the fucking hell!

First he was staring at his arm in horror. Then he was trying to stop the flow of blood with his hand. Next he gasped and flopped over on his back. He thrashed and held his arm as more and more blood squirted. It spread over his shirt and pressed pants. You could have split a grapefruit on those seams a few minutes ago, but now they just soaked up the crimson.

"Angel, man, Angel!" Kelly yelled.

Behind me, a riot had broken out.

Two of the Marines had advanced down the hallway to confront a new foe. Only this wasn't an argument. The same shit that was going on here was happening over there. Blood flowed, and lots of it. I had the stupid thought that it was going to take hours for someone to clean it all up. Screams, howls, some in pain, some in anger. Fists on skin, striking and ripping. It was worse than a riot. It was worse than any concert mosh pit I'd ever seen.

"Okay, fuck this," I said to no one in particular. I'd had enough. If anyone needed me, I'd be in main control with my people, safely locked up behind a properly dogged hatch.

Kelly took out a radio and barked orders into it. He listened to a muffled voice and then stared at the device in confusion. I paused to see if he had news.

"Say again?"

"Don't let anyone bite you. You got me, Marine? If that happens, you are dead, and then you aren't any use to anyone."

Kelly looked at me. I shook my head because it sounded crazy.

Then Angel gasped, foamed at the mouth and flopped around three or four times before his body went completely still. Kelly stared in horror as his friend died. I tried to look away from the riot that was occurring down the passageway, because it felt less real than what was happening right in front of me.

"Sir, Corporal Angel is down, Sir. He...he got bit. What do I do?"

"Shoot him in the fucking head. He isn't your buddy anymore. If you don't have a gun, then find something to bash his skull."

"Sir?"

"That's an order, Marine. You do it or I'll come down there and personally rip your head off and shit down your neck!" Kelly stared at the radio in horror. "We need to contain this before it goes any farther."

Kelly drew his sidearm and aimed it at his friend.

"Oh fuck this," I said and backed away. A riot behind or an execution ahead.

"I can't do it." Kelly put his sidearm away. The mob that had been behind us shifted momentum and was now coming toward us. One of Kelly's Marine buddies was being chased.

"Go!" the Marine yelled, then turned and opened fire. The explosions were deafening as he fired into the chaotic mass of people. Sailors and another Marine fell, but the mob kept coming. The narrow passageway created a natural bottleneck.

We fell back, Kelly pushing me while he swept his gun back and forth.

Angel picked that moment to groan and sit up. He bubbled up a putrid load of blood, his lips pulled back from his teeth in a rictus grin of pure horror. He snarled and struggled to his feet. I knocked him down but he reached for my leg and tried to bite me.

Bite me! Son of a bitch! I kicked him but pulled the blow at the last second, fearing the Marines wouldn't take too kindly to me stomping one of their own.

A snarling group came at us from the port side of the ship. They bumped into each other as they tried to maneuver the small passageway. When they got a look at us a pair moaned. Moaned! One of them howled and staggered toward me with arms raised, his hands like claws.

"Up, we need to go up!" I yelled.

Kelly looked at his friend and then back at the other Marine who had been firing. He couldn't even speak. He just shot while backing up along the passageway.

Kelly pointed his gun at Angel as the unfortunate Marine crawled toward us. Kelly aimed, but he couldn't do it. I wished I had the guts.

As our window of opportunity to escape narrowed to tens of feet, I decided that I wasn't going out screaming. I knocked Angel back to the ground and reached for his sidearm, fighting with a damn snap that secured it. Blood and drool bubbled out of Angel's mouth. Every hair on my body came to attention as he let loose with a keening noise that grew into a sound from nightmares.

"GENERAL QUARTERS GENERAL QUARTERS AND THIS IS NOT A DRILL. ABANDON SHIP. ABANDON SHIP!"

Someone howled in horror over the PA system. It might have been the captain, or maybe one of the yeomen. Either way, I was done with this shit.

"That's enough for me," I said and pointed the gun down the passageway, waving it around like I knew the first thing about weapons. Sure, I'd sunk hundreds of hours into Call of Duty but that didn't mean I knew anything about real guns.

I pulled the trigger and nothing happened.

"Come on, squid!" Kelly said and grabbed my arm. He pulled at the gun but I slapped his hand away. He looked pissed, but he'd have to put that shit on hold or we were going to get into a scuffle just before we were devoured.

"I can't leave a man behind!" the other Marine resolutely exclaimed. His name tag was covered in blood.

"Does he look like Angel? Look, man!" Kelly yelled.

Enough of this. I dove for the first ladder leading up and ran right into another mass of crazies. I aimed again, then realized there was something I'd forgotten to do and looked at the side of the gun. Sure enough, there was a safety. I flipped it, aimed again, and fired.

One of the sailors folded over as my bullet punched into him, but he quickly straightened, moving toward me and streaming blood.

Kelly moved up the ladder behind me, his buddy behind him. Great, blocked from all sides. I leapt up and barreled past the freaks, undogging the hatch leading outside. Kelly and his friend were directly on my tail as we were thrust into pre-dawn light.

"Land!" Kelly said.

I looked fore-ward and saw that the city of San Diego was coming up on us fast. What was CHENG doing down there? Had everyone decided to leave their station? Christ, the ship didn't have a chance of slowing.

"We need to get off this ship now!" I yelled over the noise of the waves.

Kelly nodded. He reached to close the hatch, but a body slipped through. Kelly lashed out and punched the moaning creeper in the face. That didn't do much more than piss him off. Kelly drew his gun again, pointed it at the man, and then shot him in the head.

"Oh shit oh shit oh shit," was all I could manage as I monkeyed with a life raft.

We had the newer MK-7s that could seat 25 but right now I couldn't even get it loose. My head pounded and I had the desire to puke up everything I'd eaten over the last 24 hours. Then I remembered the hydraulic release and hit it. The canister shot over the side but I wasn't as fast, probably because I was frozen in terror at the idea of following it.

"Are we going over?" Kelly asked.

A pair of former sailors pushed through the hatch, trailing half the crew behind them.

"Fucking zombies!" I yelled out loud, and that seemed to give me power over them. Admitting what my mind had been screaming and denying finally woke me up.

I ran to the next life raft capsule and called to Kelly and his friend.

"When I let this one rip, you guys be ready to follow it. We won't have a lot of time because that water is gonna suck. Just stick with it and follow me. Got it?" I triggered the release.

The second capsule sailed over the side and I was right behind it. The minute the capsule hit the water it exploded into a bright yellow raft. My stomach leapt into my throat as I fell toward the waves below. I crossed my arms over my chest, pinched my nose with my fingers, and clenched my asshole so I didn't get a seawater enema.

Hitting the water was like being dropped onto soggy concrete. Even with my body straight, toes pointed, I felt the impact in my chest. Cold water sucked at me. I stayed in the same position and waited to become buoyant. When "up" became apparent I kicked my legs a few times, saw light, and broke the surface with a gasp. I struck toward the raft with long strokes.

Behind me, my two Marine friends were doing their best to not drown. Kelly was the worst in his heavy vest. He tried to keep his weapon out of the water but it was already soaked.

"Come on, you pussy!" I challenged him.

Kelly did his best to give me the finger. His buddy swam up beside him and gave an assist. Together, they made it to the raft, though it was a genuine struggle with Kelly wearing that heavy combat gear. I helped haul them both in but couldn't take my eyes off of what was happening on the ship. As it sped away, sailors were jumping overboard.

Waves tossed us up and down like a yoyo. My hangover had evaporated during the chaos. I guess having a bunch of friends trying to kill you does something to the body. As we bobbed on the water, the hangover came back with a vengeance.

Kelly was still lying on his back taking in deep breaths. The other Marine stared with me toward port.

"What's your name, man?" I asked him.

"Joey Reynolds." We did introductions but neither of us looked each other in the eyes; our attention was devoted to watching our base.

"I hate the water!" Kelly sat up and followed our gaze. "Fuck me," he said.

Out of the pre-dawn chill, a layer of fog rose. After a few seconds, I realized it was smoke; San Diego was in flames. Columns rose into the air as fires grew. We were still a few miles out, but it was apparent that some kind of massive riot or catastrophic event was occurring.

The McClusky continued to steam straight toward a dock. A transport of some kind did its best to move out of the way while other ships sat silent. The white ship, whose name I couldn't make out for the life of me, must have kicked the engines into high gear. She quickly maneuvered around, front end swinging away from the dock, as the fast frigate I'd just occupied sped home.

At least the white ship managed to make it.

Men poured over the side, some following lifeboats but many with only life jackets. Others came after them: the snarling masses that had chased us right off the ship. Some of the zombies jumped, landing on sailors, while others managed to get hung up in the railing.

"There were life vests?" Kelly muttered.

A smaller ship struggled to get out of the way of the McClusky but ended up getting clipped. The sound of the two metal beasts screeching against each other was like the world's longest train wreck. But the McClusky wasn't done on her journey. She was nudged to the side; her giant propellers carried her straight past the pier to impact with the dock behind it.

"Oh my god," Reynolds said.

As if pounded by a behemoth pile-driver, the ship crumpled when her mass abruptly shifted from rear to front. Her ass-end swung around after impact and carried the rest of the ship into the dock. It took two full minutes before the McClusky was lifted into the air by a massive explosion. As the sound reached us, I hunkered down and wrapped my arms around my head, then I risked a glance over the side of the raft. The McClusky was briefly suspended on a ball of fire that destroyed the ship like it had been a tin can.

"This can't be happening," Kelly said. He reached into his pocket to pull out a cell phone, but after studying the display for a few minutes he tossed the dead device into the middle of the raft.

"Shit. I don't even have my phone," I said.

"Where is it?" Reynolds asked.

I pointed at the remnants of the ship.

#

That's enough for today. Next chance I get I'll write about Reynolds and how we established Fortress. Now I'm just sick of sitting around. Joel crashed earlier and has been snoring ever since.

I'm going to use a couple of cups of water to take a bath.

Noises outside, but not the typical crawling dead we hear wandering around out there most nights. I'll guess I'll go downstairs and check it out before I call it a night.

This is Machinist Mate First Class Jackson Creed and I am still alive.

Real Monsters

10:30 hours approximate
Location: San Diego CA - Fortress

Supplies:

- ¾ pound of Jasmine rice
- ¼ pound of dried beans
- 1 pound of that tofu-jerky
- 5 cans of tuna
- 2 cans of cat food - where the hell is Butch?
- 5 boxes of pasta
- ½ beautiful jar of spaghetti sauce
- 3 cans of various veggies
- 2 cans of mixed fruit
- 1 case of canned spinach that neither one of us had touched since we got here.

There wasn't much to do but sit around and glare at each other. Joel and I exchanged very few words.

No girls to chase. No football games to stare at. No beer to toss back. No smokes to smoke. No Xbox to play and no hot wings. Man I miss hot wings. I saw a whole bunch of seagulls the other day and all I could thing about was shooting them out of the sky so we could cook up some hot wings. I'd eat the shit out of some spicy seagull right about now.

Instead we cleaned weapons with a can of old motor oil. It wasn't pretty but it got the job done. It made me smell like a mechanic which was just like being back at home on the USS McClusky.

Just a few days ago we'd gone out and tried to raid a few houses but had little to show for it. One place had yielded a few cans of baby formula. Another had provided some aspirin and a full bottle of Tums, found buried in the back of the upstairs bathroom cabinet. We feasted on a few of those for the calcium. We dared each other to drink the baby formula. I ended up liking it but didn't tell Joel.

We went out empty-handed and that was how we came back to Fortress.

We aren't the only survivors, that's for damn sure.

Some of the homes we hit already had doors kicked open and pantries cleared. We found a bunch of empty bags one day that had contained dried beans. Next to those I found a can of condensed soup someone had punctured with a knife and drained. That had to be fun, sucking warm congealed soup without even a straw, but it beat the hell out of going hungry. Probably tasted amazing on seagull.

"Think we can shoot a few birds?"

"Are you crazy? Bring half the damn city to this location just so we can eat one of those scrawny things."

"I said a few. One scrawny bird for you and one scrawny bird for me. Probably good with the spinach."

"I'd rather eat dirt."

"Don't be so fucking morbid," I said.

Joel didn't smile.

Joel was being a jerk. He kept yelling at me about what a pain in the ass it was to watch after me when we went out. Like I knew the first goddamn thing about surviving the first goddamn zombie apocalypse.

"Fuck you, Joel Kelly. I'm good out there and you know it. Just because I don't know all the Marine hand signals like when to jerk one off doesn't mean I don't pay attention."

"Just stay low. You're big and you stick out like a sore thumb," he lectured me. "We always go in the back and we always keep an eye out for each other."

"I'm pretty sure that's what I did yesterday when I saved your ass at Ty's place." I shot back.

Joel relented with a shake of his head and went back to dour Marine looks.

I left and went upstairs to dig around in a closet again. The kid's room was filled with toys and small clothes but I figured that if I looked around long enough I'd find his stash of candy bars or Twinkies. So far I'd had no luck. He did have a toolbox filled with action figures from some super hero movie I hadn't even seen - and never would see.

Fortress was a fucking pit. An hour later, I opened the windows on the top floor but the air didn't even stir. I sat by the open portal and sucked a light breeze but then it was gone and I was miserable again.

You'd think the silence would be comforting, but it's not. All those sounds you get used to like a television or radio. Heat or running air conditioning. We had none of that. The only sound was an occasional moan, scream, or gunshot in the distance.

We'd been here for a couple of days but it felt weird living in someone else's home. I had to be careful when opening any cabinets or doors. No telling what in the hell would happen. One wrong move and a bunch of crap would be falling on the floor and all that noise would bring *them*.

Later, Joel apologized for being a dick. I nodded but didn't give in so easily.

"All you do is preach about caution but you're the first one to raise your voice out there, or worse, blow a door off its hinges. No one likes a fucking hypocrite, Joel."

"Just blowing off steam. Nothing to shoot at today so I guess words are my ammo."

"Oh that's real deep, Joel. Words as ammo. You should write a rap album."

"Are you going to go racist on me?"

"Yeah. Cause I want the only guy with a clue to think I'm a racist. Brilliant. Just shoot me in the head now."

"Like I haven't thought about it. Damn engineer. Bullets probably bounce off that thick skull."

Later, Joel attempted to be patient while teaching me survival skills. I was too pissed off to pay attention. Firing mechanism this and charging lever that. Blah blah blah.

Butch kept circling us. He whined his skinny cat ass off while we bickered. Every time I tried to reach down and scratch his scruffy head, he moved toward Joel.

Cat only had one eye and it was the evil kind and that was all he offered me.

Joel and I were both hungry and that meant one thing.

"You're the sailor. Don't you eat that shit up like Popeye?"

"You and spinach—the fuck is wrong with you? Popeye's a cartoon. What you're doing is called stereotyping."

"My black ass knows all about stereotyping." Joel shot back.

Shit. He had me there.

"I don't eat spinach. Period."

"A few days without food and I think you'll change your mind."

"Won't you?" I asked Joel.

"Nah. I'd rather starve. That shit is nasty."

We both laughed at that and the tension left the room. Funny how that happens from time to time. Other times we strut around and act like we want to kill each other.

We both knew the truth. We were rationing our supplies. If we ate our fill we'd be out of food in two days.

Butch meowed that long and forlorn mewl of his—I guess he's a he. I didn't really stop to think about checking to see if he had balls. I shushed him, so he did it again.

"If that cat brings a horde of zombies our way I'm feeding his furry butt to the first shuffler I see."

"Fucking shufflers. What are those things?"

"Dude. Do not get me started." I said.

"So many of the slow ones. Bunch of drunk bastards that can't chase worth a shit."

"Yeah but get enough of them together...I remember the base," I said and thought, with sadness, of Reynolds.

"Anyway. The shufflers."

"They don't move like people and they don't move like your garden variety Z. They got that weird step and how the hell do they creep along on their hands and feet?"

Joel got on all fours and tried to duplicate the move. It was hilarious. He tried to stay on his hands and feet and move but he kept straining to stay low to the ground. After ten or fifteen seconds he gave up and rolled over on his back.

"That shit is insane," he said, panting.

"Thanks for making my day." I laughed and clapped him on the shoulder.

"Five minutes. Let's get in the war."

"A war indicates there's an enemy out there that is shooting back. So far it's been pretty one-sided, Joel."

"Should be an easy one to win," Joel said and got up to strap on his tactical gear.

I nodded and went to gather up my stuff. I couldn't help but wonder what we'd do if we won.

The first time we went out was at night. It didn't matter that we snuck around like a couple of special-needs ninjas. The thing about the Z's was that it was easier to see them than worry about them seeing us. Besides, we only had the one NVG and Joel wore that because he was the goddamn action hero, leaving me stumbling into stuff.

The next time we went out it was early morning. We left just as dawn was burning away and there was that low mist that hung around. It was creepy under normal circumstances but add in a bunch of Z's and it's like some nightmare movie. You just don't walk around in that soup, see a dude missing half his fucking face, and act like it's a normal day.

I'd already shrugged into my BDU's, wearing them over a thick flannel shirt left by the owners of the house. The material was hot but I felt a little bit safer having it cover my arms. One bite was all it took, and if this kept me from losing some skin, I could put up with it. I'd feel even better if I had duct tape wrapped around each sleeve but then I'd have to cut my way out. Besides, I'd worked in an engine room for years and the thick layer was just shy of uncomfortable. See that, grunge rockers? This shit is functional.

We went over the side and then stashed the ladder. The front was locked up and hammered shut. I straightened our "looters will be shot dead" sign, and then we moved out.

We crept around a few houses we'd already searched. Others had boarded up windows and barred doors so we didn't bother. As much as I'd like to say we talked with other survivors that just wasn't the case.

In the movies everyone goes into hyper survival mode and shoots, rapes, or pillages with glee. In reality, we'd found that most survivors just wanted to be left alone. Everyone was distrustful and that was fine with me. I didn't want to worry about feeding any more mouths.

We moved onto a new section of town about half a mile from our current location. Joel wore his combat gear and had the NYFD ball cap on backwards. His AR-15 swept in every direction. We had a map back at Fortress and Joel kept marking off sections we'd explored. This wasn't one of them. Virgin territory to us. Probably Z-infested and picked over but we had to get lucky eventually.

There were older homes here and we were far enough from the Naval base that I hoped we weren't busting into other sailor's houses and stealing their shit. Yeah, I realize that most of them were probably dead but it still felt like the wrong thing to do.

We came across the home at the end of a cul-de-sac. The place was newer or remodeled and really out of place in the ghetto that made up most of this neighborhood. That's what Joel called it, but it was a lot nicer than where I grew up in Detroit. My school was so rough, the only things that kept me from getting my ass kicked, consistently, were my fists and my size. I'd been a bully then, because it was expected, but I never liked it. Much.

"How about this place?" I whispered near Joel's ear.

He was crouched behind a beat up sedan and going over his rifle. When he wasn't shooting at Z's, Joel was inspecting his weapon. I had my .45 M45A1 holstered but my pipe wrench was at hand. Bring on the Z's. I was ready to bash some heads. I was the silent partner, as Joel liked to put it. Point me in the direction of a few of the dead and I'd take them down with a swing or two.

A group of Z's moved one block west of our location. They were a nasty bunch that probably turned during the first few days of the outbreak. Dressed in rags, they had that starved look with sunken cheeks and hollow eye sockets. The leader had a steady but slow gait, thanks to a broken foot. His face was caved in and one eye socket was covered in dried blood and a fuck load of maggots.

"I'm gonna puke," Joel whispered.

"Don't start cause I'll be right behind you. Hard to shoot Z's when you're tossing your lunch."

"Good Christ in heaven. How is something like that even on its feet?

Every time he staggered forward, a couple of bugs fell off his face and he nearly lost his footing. Then this decayed dude would right himself, swing his good leg again and stumble forward. The four behind him weren't in much better shape. A woman in a jogging suit was missing most of her face but at least it wasn't filled with maggots. Just gore and stuff that might have been bone.

Another group followed and this bunch was much fresher. When I write about fresh Z's you have to understand that there's a whole host of the dead out there. Sure, the first bunch were old and rotted. We saw a lot of those. When the body dies, or comes down with whatever shit virus had killed the world, the body rots. Then stuff starts to fall off. The parts that are left reek like the worst rancid meat you ever smelled. Man, I just can't describe it. Go to a dump in the summer and walk right to the center. I guarantee it won't be as bad as these things.

So the second batch were a lot fresher. The rot was setting in but they were walking and jawing. That is, their mouths kind of unhinged and their tongues stuck out. If one of these Z's fell, odds were good that a hunk of meat was hitting the ground, maybe a piece of a kneecap or an elbow. The biggest problem was how fast they were. Take a week-old rotted Z. They can't chase worth a shit. A day-old slugger? They're almost as fast as a live person. Get ten of those together and it's a hell of a bad day.

They moved around the first group, seemingly oblivious to the rotters. Then they pressed on toward the end of the block, but not before one whipped its head around and stared right at our hiding spot. It shuffled around in a circle then looked toward the sky and let out a moan. Milky white eyes settled on us again, but they weren't aware we were in the bushes.

It was a long five minutes while we waited for the second batch to round the corner and move out of eyesight. One of the rotters, however, picked a spot on the ground and stared at it. That's when I saw the figure dart around a house next to the one we were trying to raid. They were dressed in black and wore a ski mask. They had a bunch of knives strapped to their chest and a handgun of some sort. They took up a position in the shadow of the green rambler and froze in place.

Joel didn't move, either, and that meant I was a statue. After a few minutes the figure moved off. He or she did not even look in our direction. Joel and I sighed at about the same time and then shot each other disapproving looks.

We moved around the house and checked the windows. Locked.

The house's front door was closed and that was a good sign. Too often we came across front doors and windows smashed in, and that meant someone had already picked the place clean.

"This place looks deserted but it might be like fortress. Guy in there with a shotgun would take us down pretty easily," Joel whispered.

"Should we knock?" I asked.

"Yeah. You go knock and if you get shot I'll know to go back to Fortress."

"Let's scout the back."

Joel clapped my back. "See, I'll make a warrior out of you yet."

"Be better if you could make some damn hot wings," I said.

The house had an older pine fence with most of a finish. Looks like the apocalypse put a stop to that. A can of wood stain lay off to one side. It was kicked over and empty. I moved to peek over the top and didn't see a dog waiting to chase us toward our recently departed zombie horde.

Joel pushed at the gate but it didn't budge. I slipped my hand over the top and felt around until I found a release, then slid the gate open. We crept into the back yard with Joel Kelly in the lead. He dashed to the edge of the home and then crouched with his AR covering the backyard. He didn't move for a full fifteen seconds and then slipped around the back.

I had to wonder what I'd do if I was, say, lounging around in my back yard in a pair of boxers and someone crept along the side of my house dressed in tactical gear and carrying an assault rifle. I'd probably shit myself and then offer them everything in my wallet.

Joel moved into the yard and I followed. Then he stopped, dropped to a crouch, and gestured for me to get down. I complied with his instructions and faded toward a small maple. It was one of the healthiest trees I'd seen and that worried me. Did someone live here? Someone with the means to take care of their shrubs? I shook my head. It was probably just the unseasonably warm autumn we were experiencing. It really looked healthy. It was garnet and willowy but didn't provide a lot of cover, especially for my BDU's

Joel motioned and I followed his hands. There was a pile of something near the sliding glass door. I shook my head because I couldn't believe it.

There had to be fifteen or twenty bodies in various states of decay. Flies buzzed around in a swarm of black. The sound was enough to drive me nuts.

The smell was horrendous.

All of the bodies were female and all were nude. Clothing was lain on top of them but arranged in a garish way, like they were some kind of clowns. The woman on top was probably in her fifties when she died and not exactly the spitting image of a super model. She was a mom, or had been, but now she was dead and her face was covered in someone's crude attempt at makeup. Bright red hooker lipstick rode her dry lips. Her mouth was open and she didn't have any teeth, just a bunch of bloody holes.

"The fuck?" Joel said exactly what I was thinking, except I was thinking it over and over in my head.

Another woman was much younger but most of her face was smashed in. Her neck was cocked at an impossible angle and I feared that if I touched her the head would loll toward me and her eyes would snap open.

"Were they all Z's before they were killed?"

"I don't know, man. I don't know." Joel shook his head.

I wondered if he was thinking what I was thinking. That some sick fuck needed to die for this. Take a Z down, man. Don't be a fucking asshole.

I pointed at the house and Joel followed my finger and stared for a full half minute.

"We should go somewhere else."

"Yeah. We should. Stay here and back me up."

"Dammit. We should leave," I whispered.

"I want to know what's up," Joel said. His eyes didn't look inquisitive. They looked pissed.

"Going in blazing?" I asked.

"I'm not stupid."

"Yeah, okay, Mr. Marine."

Joel puckered his lips like he was preparing to blow me a Marine kiss and then shot me the finger. He crept to the edge of the house and lowered himself next to the sliding glass door. He took a quick peek and then dropped back a few feet. No one blasted. Good enough start.

Joel took another look and this time lingered. He stared and stared and then he motioned for me to join him.

"Break it. Break the fucking door." He nodded at my giant wrench.

"Really?"

"Dude. Just do it." His eyes burned so I shrugged and took a swing.

Just before the wrench shattered the window, I saw why.

When the glass hit the patio and floor, I stood in place while my brain tried to make sense of the scene.

Then my face flushed and my blood boiled.

Joel went in yelling.

"Down, get the fuck down! I am not messing around! If you make one wrong move I'll erase you!"

The man with his pants around his ankles looked at us and then slowly raised his arms.

I took a step toward him with the wrench raised and murder in my blood. I wanted to beat this guy until he was pulp and then toss him on the pile outside.

His living room was a mess of old clothes and empty food containers. There were so many empty packs of crackers and candy bars I wouldn't be able to take a step without something crackling under foot.

Someone had spray-painted the words "MONSTER KEN" on one of the walls in blood red paint.

The house was dark and warm. It reeked of garbage and blood. It smelled like the dead. On top of that, the guy before us smelled like he hadn't showered in a month.

The worst part was the girl. She was bent over the arm of a light brown leather couch that was stained with blood. Her naked legs moved but that was all. Her arms were tied at the wrist, behind her back. She moaned but couldn't move her head because a rope had been tied around her neck and stretched to the other side of the couch and then tied to something.

"Notmenotmenotmenotme! It's Ken. He's the monstermonster monsterman! Ken's coming back. Not me not me not fucking me."

"Shut up or I'll end you." Joel's voice was full of barely-controlled rage.

I didn't say anything because every fiber of my being wanted to crush in his skull. I clenched the wrench so hard my hand trembled.

"Ken did Ken did Ken did," the guy rambled on and on under his breath.

"Let her go," I said.

"Can't. Can't do it. Can't until Ken gets here but he said I could take a turn. See? He said it was cool so it's cool and everything's cool. So cool." He touched the girl's back and ran his hands over her waist, then gave her butt a squeeze.

"Rapist." Joel pronounced it like a death sentence and raised his weapon.

"Can't rape the dead." The man cackled.

I backed up a step and tried to keep my lunch down.

"What the fuck!" Joel said and centered the man in his sights.

Then something crashed down the hallway and we both froze.

'Ken!" the guy screeched, and that was enough for me.

I hit him so hard he probably didn't even feel it, just saw a blast of light.

A figure dashed across the hallway into the kitchen. Joel dropped and fired a few rounds.

I dropped behind the couch and tried to pick a spot to crawl toward. The woman's eyes settled on mine and she snarled even though she was gagged. She couldn't have been more than eighteen years old. She wore the same shade of lipstick as the bodies outside.

Another figure appeared in the hallway but it moved slowly. Joel didn't stop to ask questions; he just shot the person in the chest. Then another shape appeared.

"Out!" Joel said and rose to cover me.

A pair of shots came from the direction of the first figure, now in the kitchen, and struck the wall. The bullets were high but they were enough to tell me that I didn't like being shot at.

I went flat as Joel backed up and fired a few more rounds.

This was beyond our thirty-second battle drill. We should be hauling ass. I tried to shimmy along the floor but realized it would leave my big ass exposed and stayed low.

"When I fire, you move. Got it?" Joel didn't waste any time and ripped half a dozen rounds at the indistinct shape in the kitchen. Then he dropped the creeper coming up the hallway, but there was one more behind them.

At least we hit whoever was shooting at us. The person grunted and then fell. Joel aimed in his direction but was stopped because of the fresh hell that was about to enter my living nightmare.

The shuffler moved faster than anything alive. It didn't even pause to check out the naked girl bent over the couch, it just came at us like a rabid dog. It snarled and sputtered with a sound that was like coughing. It ran at Joel, took a bullet to the shoulder and didn't stop.

The guy in the kitchen must have figured this was his chance. He peeked around the corner and for the first time I got a look at him. It was the same person I'd seen earlier wearing a ski mask.

I dropped my wrench and tugged the big .45 out of my holster, checked the safety, raised it, and shot at the guy.

He ducked back around the corner. His handgun came out and he emptied a magazine into the room. We tried to duck, but the shuffler was on us.

He went for Joel with a leap that barely cleared the couch. I risked grabbing my wrench and then swung it around. I missed, but it was better than accidentally shooting Joel.

They both crashed through the remains of the glass door and went down in a heap. Joel abandoned his assault rifle and went for his side arm but his hand was batted aside. He tried to throw a punch while getting up and was tackled. Then he was out of sight.

I lifted the handgun and fired back at the man in black out of fear and panic. I had to rescue Joel. He was a tough and fast son of a bitch, but he was facing a shuffler all alone. I fired wildly and made for the screen door but bullets zipped over my head.

"Ken. That's a shuffler. Let me kill it or we're both done."

Another form appeared in the shadows of the hallway.

"I know. I brought them for you." A man's voice cackled. "Think you can sneak into my house? My house? I brought them."

Boom! The shot ripped through the space over my head.

"For you!"

Then he fired several more times while I hugged the floor. Made it my best friend.

I curled up in a ball and wondered if I was going to be Z-chow in a minute.

A grunt from the outside made me snap my head in that direction. Was Joel dead? Did the shuffler get him? I had to get out there and I had to get out there now.

The form that had appeared in the doorway staggered toward me. Ken laughed. Monster Ken — what a perfect name for this asshole.

The fresh Z was a large woman in her thirties. Her face was a mess of bite marks but her guts hung around her waist. I lifted the gun to shoot at her but it clicked empty. Great. I'd forgotten Joel Kelly's rules. I rolled against the side of the couch, put my hand on the cushion to steady myself, and was almost bitten by the girl strapped there.

Reloading was a cinch thanks to hundreds of practice runs. I silently vowed to thank my Marine friend.

I fired four rounds in Ken's direction while he fired back. The space between us had to be less than fifteen feet, but I was the lucky one. Ken grunted and then screamed. The Z in the hallway turned her head and moaned in his direction, then moved toward him.

I rushed out the door, expecting the worse.

The shuffler was on his back in the pile of the dead. He twitched, then rolled over and cackled. His hand went to his mouth while he considered me. The man's hair hung in clumps over his forehead. His face was covered in blood and gore. His clothing was just as soaked in crimson.

He bit off one of his fingers while he stared from milky eyes that had the oddest hint of green. It was like they glowed with some otherworldly intelligence.

Joel staggered to his feet and for a moment I feared he'd been bitten and was already turning, but he pulled his Marine combat knife. Then he took a step toward the shuffler. Oh, I get it. This was one of those Marine things that I should stay out of. Joel was only interested in finishing the monster.

The shuffler leapt. Sure, I could have let Joel Kelly, Marine superman take the shuffler, and with any luck Joel would come out the victor. But I'd had enough of this entire scouting mission. I swung hard and caught the shuffler in the side, changing his reality in mid leap from forward momentum to crushed bones and flailing limbs. The creature howled and fell into an awkward tangle.

Joel advanced but I lifted the .45 and shot the son of a bitch in the head. Twice.

Fuck that guy.

Joel staggered into me and got an arm around my shoulder.

"If you bite me I'm going to be really fucking disappointed, Joel Kelly."

"He didn't get me. He just hit me hard enough to make me see stars. Thanks, man. I didn't think I'd be able to take him."

"So what, you just judo-threw him or something?"

"Got my gun around and cracked him upside the head. He fell back on the pile, but goddamn – that thing was fast. And strong."

"So this is my reward? A Marine hug. If you kiss me I'm going to hit you with my really big wrench."

Joel laughed and punched me in the shoulder hard enough to leave a bruise. Such a kidder, that guy.

"I think Monster Ken is still alive in there."

"Yeah?"

I grinned and went in but kept low in case Ken'd gotten lucky with the dead lady.

The only sounds were his calls for help.

I advanced quietly on the kitchen and poked my head in to see even more squalor. There were wrappers everywhere. Empty water bottles. Rotting meat in the sink. What kind of meat, I had no interest in discovering.

The rapist twitched. Shit, didn't I kill that son of a bitch?

Joel came in and covered me. He pointed his assault rifle at the woman on the couch but I shook my head.

"Enough shooting for one day. We gotta move, buddy. Our thirty seconds ended about five minutes ago."

"What about dickless in there?"

I poked my head around the corner and saw that the Z was on top of Ken. She had knocked him down and he must have hit something hard because his right arm was at a bad angle. I ducked in and snagged his gun. It was a Sig Sauer P229 and that seemed like a hell of a sexy gun.

"How's it going, Ken?" I asked.

He turned blazing eyes on me as he tried to fight off the woman. She got her mouth into his shoulder and ripped up. Ken screamed.

"Don't be such a fucking pansy," I said and went back to the living room.

The guy I hit twitched and one eye opened. The other had been crushed in by my wrench.

Joel grabbed the rapist and dragged him while I untied the woman and led her into the kitchen by the rope. She was covered in wounds and barely put up a struggle. She didn't have any clothing on, but the last thing I wanted to do was look at the twin horrors that were her tits.

"Hey Joel. It's an orgy," I said and pushed her toward Ken.

Joel dragged the other rapist in and tossed him onto the pile. The naked girl went at him. She ripped up his shirt and dug her mouth into his soft belly. Even with his head half bashed in, the man managed to open his eyes and start muttering "no no no" over and over again.

"Hansi," Ken yelled and reached for his friend.

Movement at the front of the house. I risked a look to confirm it was the faster pack we'd seen a few minutes ago right outside the house. So Ken really had led a bunch of Z's here just to protect his home. Did he think he'd be able to overpower them and us when it was all over? Was Ken really enough of a Z survivor to take us all down?

Joel pointed at the back door and I nodded. We hustled and slipped out, hurrying past the pile of dead. We found the side of the house and hid next to the fence. A minute later the street cleared, so we moved out.

Behind me, the screams went on for a long time.

I couldn't stop smiling.

###

We crouched near Fortress and watched for a good ten minutes. Joel kept his eye on the house while I watched out back. The backyard we'd picked for our reconnaissance had a kid's playground. There was a trampoline with a body on it. The sides were covered in mesh so no one would fall out. Now it was a weird grave for the man that had blown his brains out while lying on it.

The yard also had a bunch of tall bushes we frequently used for cover.

A few days ago we'd gone into this home to look for supplies. We'd only turned up a few small bags of dried beans on the top shelf of the pantry. Someone had beaten us to this place.

We'd found the family in one room. A woman, presumably the mother, had been lain out on the bed with a pair of small bodies. The covers were pulled up and cloths placed over their faces. Someone had shot all three of them. My money was on the guy on the trampoline. After that, we never went into the house again. It was a mausoleum now.

Satisfied that no one was raiding Fortress, we went home.

"Empty-handed," I muttered as we used a few precious baby wipes to clean up back at Fortress.

I lit a Sterno can and contemplated the spinach.

"I'll eat one if you eat one," Joel challenged.

"Christ. I guess it's come to this."

The cans took a few minutes to warm up but not so long to devour. Tasted like shit but it was better than being belly up at Ken's house. Joel was smart and suggested adding a little bit of our precious supply of rice to the containers for the carbs. My gut rolled over but I was hungry enough to ignore the taste. The house hadn't had a lot of food when we claimed it, but we'd found a box of chicken bouillon cubes and they'd gone in just about everything we attempted to cook.

"What the hell, man?" I finally spoke after we sat in silence for a few moments.

"Don't even get me started."

"Who does that shit? Who?"

"Monster Ken."

"Yeah. Well, Monster Ken is a real monster now. I hope that jerk is wandering around tomorrow so we can kill him again."

"We didn't actually finish our sweep yesterday. Head back?" Joel grinned.

"I like how you think, buddy," I smiled and hit Joel in the arm hard enough to leave a bruise.

He choked back a gasp and then looked stoic.

I went to bed with a smile on my face for the first time in days.

I guess the fucking zombie apocalypse could be worse.

This is Machinist Mate First Class Jackson Creed and I am still alive.

NIGHT TERRORS

19:40 hours approximate
Location: San Diego CA - Fortress

Why in the hell did we ever leave? There is a reason I named this place Fortress and leaving it was never a good idea. Unfortunately, Joel made a very convincing argument that we needed to return to the San Diego Naval base for supplies. He used small words like "we need food and ammo, you dumb squid."

Joel never listened to my ideas. I'd made a few but I was sick and tired of the Marine giving me a ration of shit for every single one of them.

"Let's go raid cars."

"Bad idea," he'd say. "Could be the wrong car is full of dead."

Could be? Sure, but we're good at killing them. Real good. If there was an Olympics held today for how to kill Z's, we'd at least win the bronze.

"Let's go find a house with an abandoned hot tub so we can take a bath."

"Then we'd be caught with our pants down." Jesus, he could be such a drag.

"Let's go find other survivors."

"They'll just steal our stuff or maybe try to eat us." On second thought, that one actually made sense.

"Christ, Joel. No one's going to eat us."

"Not yet. Wait until they haven't eaten for a few days," he said ominously. I dropped it.

Anyway, I would do my usual list of food supplies but I'm too pissed off right now so I'll do it tomorrow. There'll be less to write about by then if Roz has her say.

Yeah – Roz.

24 October, 20:08 hours approximate
Location: San Diego CA

Weapons:

- 1 AR-15
- 3 30 round mags
- 97 Rounds of 5.56 ammo
- 1 Colt M45A1 Handgun
- 42 Rounds of .45 ammo
- 1 Sig Sauer P229
- 14 rounds of 9mm ammo
- 1 very large fucking wrench
- 1 12 gauge Remington pump action shotgun
- 4 12 gauge shells

The other night I finished up my entry regarding how Joel, Reynolds, and I escaped from the USS McClusky. As best as I could tell, of the 178 souls on board, only three of us managed to get off the ship before it smashed into the pier and exploded.

It was late and I was about to blow out my candle for the night when I heard something below. Night gets real quiet except for the occasional helicopter in the distance or an airplane too high to see. Every time I heard those I wondered if it was our time to die. I was surprised they hadn't already nuked this dead fucking cesspool.

The noise was different than the Z's that sometimes shamble by. This was more like someone on the move. Someone that has a purpose. But it was gone as soon as I'd convinced myself to get up and check it out.

Eventually I fell asleep but had my wrench within reach and the pistol tucked under my pillow. I may be one paranoid mother fucker but I'm also one very alive mother fucker.

Today we did the same thing as yesterday—broke down our weapons and cleaned them. I even took a cloth to my wrench head and got most of the blood, hair, and brain matter off of it.

After we'd bitched and bickered and then managed not to kill each other, I went to bed and considered rolling a joint. I didn't, though, because as much as I love to give the Marine shit, I didn't really want to let him down. And if I got high and some of those things got in here I might just giggle my ass off while I looked for something to kill them with.

I was dozing when I heard it again.

I was sure I'd heard voices and then something got knocked over. Shit! Now I knew I wasn't crazy. I heard more voices and decided that if we had looters alerted to our location I should just go out there and scare them away. Now how fucking stupid is that? What was I going to do? Go out there dressed like a horrible monster? Those are a dime a dozen now. I'd be like "BOO!" And they'd be like "SHOOT IT!"

I felt around in the dark until I located my lighter, struck a flame, then fumbled around for my shirt. Joel had left his pair of NVG's hanging on the wall so I grabbed those and slid them over my head. He'd be pissed if he found me wearing his toys. Joel always worried about how much juice the batteries had remaining. I worried about being killed by those fucking things out there, so I guess that made us kind of even.

Switching on the NVG's brought the world into shades of green. I moved to a window and scanned the ground below. There were a few trees out there but most were so dry from the heat, they didn't even have leaves. Bushes were easy to pick out. I could look out without the goggles and see a dozen things that scared the shit out of me.

I hovered for a few minutes just watching the ground a story below. When nothing materialized, I moved to the other side of the house. Joel was still snoring away behind his cracked door. I looked in and found him sprawled out on the mattress. The first thing Joel did when we took over the house was drag the mattress off the bed. I asked him why and he said he felt safer.

"A Marine scared of things under the bed?" I'd asked.

"Hey man. There are a lot of things out there to be scared about. This is one less."

With the Night Vision Goggle over my eye I was able to move around the dark house with ease. I checked the other side of the house but didn't see anything. I hovered by a window and listened for a good fifteen minutes but there was nothing.

Maybe I was just going stir crazy.

It took a half-second to wake up Joel. He was on his feet and reaching for his assault rifle so fast it was like he had a giant spring built in his ass. His room smelled like sweat and oil. That would be Joel and his best friend, an assault rifle.

"Shh," I whispered. "I think someone's outside."

"Just leave the dead fucks be. They'll wander away. Now let a brother get some shut eye."

"I don't know. It's so quiet, maybe I was just hearing things, but these things sounded like voices."

"Shit," Joel said. "Lemme grab the NVGs."

I handed them over. Good thing it was dark so I didn't have to put up with a dirty look.

Joel grumped around doing Marine shit while I waited. I did a check of my side arm and ran through ammo, slide, and safety positioning. I had a full mag of 7 rounds and one in the chamber. One more mag went into a pocket and I dropped a handful of shells into my other. My lucky .45 round was still in its place right next to my hip. All I needed was my wrench and I was ready to bash some heads.

###

Going outside meant navigating off the deck. There's no other way in unless someone has a tool that can bust the front door off. We picked this place because it had one main entrance. We filled the entryway with crap like a sofa and then piled a few bodies on top. It made for a gruesome entry.

Next chapter I'll write about Fortress, promise. That way, if my corpse is found, readers will understand what a pain in the ass this place was to secure and appreciate all the effort we went through.

You're welcome.

The only dead that stopped by were ignored. If they got persistent Joel and I would drop cinder blocks on their heads. The blocks were attached to ropes so we could pull them back up. We had a pool going on weekly kills and I was up by three. The best part was trying to get their attention just before the block struck. They'd look up with that blank face, those white eyes, and then SPLAT!

Joel went out and stared into the dark for so long I thought he'd fallen asleep standing up. I waited and went over my gun again and again.

Joel had taught me to treat it like a girl with a rocking body. You want to know every inch of her because you can't dream about her later unless you've been hands-on for hours.

"There's no one out here."

"Yeah. Now. There was a few minutes ago."

"You been hitting the ganja?" Joel asked.

"Not today. I swear, man, I heard something."

"They're gone now. Get some sleep. We need to leave in a couple of hours."

"Yeah. I'll do my best."

When Joel left I dragged my mattress next to the sliding glass door and left it cracked open so the breeze rolled over me, but also so I could hear anyone approaching. The thin bit of breeze helped, but I was a long way from anything resembling sleep. I tossed and turned as I strained to hear anything besides the occasional moan of one of the Z's wandering around in the dark.

Finally I closed my eyes and drifted off, dreaming that I was back on the McClusky and the crew had been replaced by a team of bikini models all named Helen. Every one of them.

Joel's hand on my shoulder tore me out of sleep.

"Ugh," I muttered.

"Mission time," he said and moved away.

I was tempted to just go back to sleep. Fuck exploration, it was the middle of the goddamn night. I sat up and rubbed what felt like sand out of my eyes.

While I suited up in my engineer overalls, Joel stood to the side of the deck entrance and scanned the area. He was already dressed in his combat gear. He checked his pockets one more time, pulling magazines out to do a visual inspection by the light of the moon. Satisfied, he stuffed them back into pouches at his chest and side, then secured them by pressing flaps in. Early on, we'd learned the hard way that the crackle of a Velcro pocket could bring a pack in seconds.

Joel dragged the ladder out and lowered it to the ground, moving it around until he was satisfied it had a good hold on the ground. He slung his AR-15 over his shoulder and then went down the ladder while I trained the .45 around the area. When he was on the ground, he covered for me.

We hid the ladder under a pile of brush and dragged a pair of rotting corpses on top to keep prying eyes on other things.

Our destination was the naval base. Joel had wanted to return for the past week, but the Z's in the area had been too heavy. After some scouting earlier today we determined that it might be safe to slip in, find some warehouse he knew about, commandeer a car, and get the fuck back to dodge, all before the night was over. We really needed to load up on ammo and maybe another weapon or two. If we got stuck with our current weapon pool, I doubted we'd be able to shoot our way out of a wet paper bag before we ran out of rounds.

Fucking zombies. I hate them.

Joel scouted ahead while I brought up the rear. I grumbled but a look from the Marine reminded me that it was time to get serious. One misstep out in this world and we'd be dead meat.

I did find that with night came something amazing. Cold air. It rolled off the water and reminded me of what it was like before we ended up stuck in Fortress. Going out like this was familiar. We'd already done it half a dozen times and we were still alive. The other thing that I found was the smell of decay. It was everywhere. Trash and bodies rotting in the sun made for a disgusting reek that clung to everything.

The idea was to remain quiet. As quiet as a sleeping baby. Any loud noises and you were likely to call in a pack of the dead. Not that they actually traveled together, because they had no thoughts in their heads. They reacted to some bizarre need to find live flesh. I liked my flesh right where it was — on my bones.

Joel stopped alongside a house and then faded against the wall. He moved around the corner with me right behind. Joel held up a hand and I stopped in my tracks. He did something with his NVG's and then motioned for me to advance.

I crept around the corner and stopped as well.

Joel signaled for me to creep forward, then stopped me when I was a few feet away. He turned and put his fingers to his lips. Joel slipped the NVG's off his head and handed them to me. I slid my handgun into the holster, took the glasses and slipped them over my head. He had his eyes closed but pointed at the garage. Curious about what the hell he wanted to show me, I moved toward it in the half crouch I'd seen him pull off many times. He made it look easy but I was a lot bigger. Shit was not easy.

The world jumped to life in hues and shades of green. The house was a single story rambler with the remains of a broken fence scattered all over the lawn. The front door hung off its hinges and a corpse lay on the small concrete patio. Even in the pale light of the moon, I could tell that his form had been torn to shreds. A rifle lay next to him. Other bodies littered the patio. It appeared the guy had done his best to fend for his home, but in the end, the Z's got him.

The garage door was stuck half-open but that wasn't what made me freeze in my tracks. It was the sounds.

If I didn't know any better I'd have guessed there was some kind of feast underway in the garage. Maybe a barbecue in San Diego. Just another night for some civilian (or more likely, military) family.

What I saw was anything but.

I lowered myself to a crouch and moved my head around the corner of the house. The walls were stacked with boxes and some old furniture had been pushed into corners. A bike hung from the ceiling. That's where "normal" ended.

In the center of the room sat four figures. They were dressed in rags and slicked with something wet; even with the NVG's, I knew it was blood. One gazed up at the wall from its meal. I stifled a gasp when I realized the Z had been chewing on his own fingers. One of the four was an overweight woman missing most of her clothes. She sat and gibbered to herself while also chewing on the ends of her fingers. I don't mean nibbled, either. She had literally devoured them. A couple of teens rounded out the family from hell.

It was so absurd that all I wanted to do was go in and shoot each one in the damn head.

I ducked back around the corner and shrugged my shoulders at Joel. He leaned in close.

"That shit is fucked up," he whispered.

I dragged my finger across my neck and shrugged again. Joel shook his head.

He motioned toward my head so I took the NVG's off and handed them over. As Joel grasped them, I heard someone approach from the other side of the house. I dropped to a crouch while Joel fumbled with the glasses.

A figure entered the yard from the west side and was doing nothing to mask his sounds. With the glasses off it took a few seconds to adjust to the natural light of the moon. I drew the Colt M45A1 as quietly as possible, lifted it with two hands, and aimed.

The person went to the corpse in the middle of the yard and picked up the rifle. They looked it over then felt around in the corpse's pockets and came up with shells. The sound of them being loaded into the shotgun was like firecrackers popping in the still of night.

Joel crouched next to the side of the house and aimed the assault rifle. Shit! Shit! Shit! If we got into a firefight with someone, the Z's would be here in a heartbeat.

I moved to his side and looked around the corner. The person lifted the gun and came toward us. Before we could react, the person walked into the garage and the shotgun sounded like a cannon blast. The gun was pumped and boomed again. Feet scrambled on concrete and the form backed out in a hurry. There were three of them on the person, who got off one more shot.

"Fuckers! You killed my family!" she screamed. Yeah – she.

She backed up a few more steps and racked another shell into the gun. She fired but ended up clipping one of the Z's arms. Part of the arm disappeared, leaving shreds of clothing and flesh.

They advanced on her.

She backed up, pumping the shot gun over and over again, but she must have been empty. When she cleared the garage with the three Z's nearly on her, I broke from cover. I slid my handgun back into its holster and hefted my wrench. The last Z stumbled out of the garage and I was horrified to see it was one of the kids. She staggered and moaned but didn't have a lot of momentum. Then I saw why. She was dragging one of her feet at an angle that was impossible for a normal person. It was definitely broken, a gruesome fracture with the bone sticking out, but little Miss Sunshine didn't care.

I moved behind her in a couple of steps and brought the wrench around in an arc that ended with her head. She dropped like a rock and I was rewarded with a pile of brain matter on the end of wrench head.

Then I hit something on the ground, a rock or broken piece of crap from the house, and stumbled. My ankle twisted under me and I almost went down.

One of the Z's turned on me and it was all I could do to fend him off. The guy was almost as big as me and dressed in khaki shorts with the remains of a black t-shirt clinging to his body. I took his attack and tried to turn him away by using his own momentum to toss him aside, but my foot screamed in agony and I ended up in a heap.

Fucker was fresh dead. He wasn't like the slower corpses that had been hanging out for a few days. This guy was quick and his teeth gnashed in toward my shoulder like a viper. I got the wrench in the way and smacked him aside. I managed to get an elbow in and hit him hard enough to roll the fucker off me. Jesus Christ! He smelled horrible – and I've worked around sailors for most of my life, so that should tell you something.

I swung the wrench again, but I panicked and it crashed into his chest. Any normal man would have been crushed. It barely fazed this dead fuck.

The girl must have figured out how to get her shot gun functioning because it boomed again. I swore, hoping she didn't mistake me for one of the dead. I rolled to my side and almost got my hands on the ground to pick myself up. Then I felt a claw on my shirt as the guy pulled me back down. I rolled and got a boot up. I lifted it high in the air and hit the Z again, but just in the chest, and all that did was knock him flat.

Where the hell was Joel?

"Get out of the fucking way!" Joel kept his voice low.

"About time!" I tried to echo his tone but panic rode my voice and I may have sounded like a scared six-year-old girl.

The Z grabbed my leg but I kicked free and rolled again. Joel's boots came into view and then the AR-15 fired. The Z was blown onto his back.

One more shot to the head and the guy didn't move again.

I got to my feet and limped after Joel, ankle aching with every step.

"Are they dead?" The girl with the shotgun approached. She didn't even look us in the face; she just studied the corpses on the ground.

"Yeah, all dead - need to clear this area before more arrive." Joel said.

"I'll stay here and hold them back. Thanks for the assist." She said. Her voice had a slight Latino accent.

"Come with us," I said impulsively. Or was it impulsive? Were we just supposed to leave another survivor behind while we made an escape?

Joel grabbed my shirt sleeve and tugged.

"We can't leave her."

"If she wants to stay, let her," he said near my ear, but she was probably able to hear him.

"We can't leave someone behind like that."

"Since when did you grow a fucking sense of morality? We ain't got the supplies for another survivor."

"Just go," the girl said. "That's my dad on the lawn. The eaters in the garage killed everyone. There's nothing left."

"Oh, for fucks sake." Joel said and stared at both of us.

The sound of something shuffling down the street sent a chill down my neck. I looked for shapes.

I grabbed the girl's hand and tugged her close. "Just until we get free; then you can do whatever you want."

"I don't care. I just don't care anymore. I got nothing," she repeated.

"I need help, okay? I can't run because I sprained my ankle."

"Fine. Fuck! You helped me, so I'll help you." She lifted my arm and put it around her shoulders.

Joel swore a few more times and then took point. I gimped along behind him, holding the girl close.

"I'm Jackson," I told her as I trained the gun all over the place.

"I'm Roz. Jackson your first or last name?"

"First. Jackson Creed."

"Okay, man. Now that we got introductions out of the way, why don't you shut the fuck up so we don't get swarmed?"

"Me? You're the one that came in with guns blazing. If it weren't for my wrench you'd be one of them by now."

"Keep your wrench in your pants and keep that gun aimed. Where we going anyway?"

"Fortress, I guess."

"Fortress?"

"It's just what we call home. Do you have any food?"

"Lots in my house. Before we were overrun we had a big stash."

"How'd you get overrun?"

"They were making a lot of noise. Dad snuck out to see what it was. One of them saw him and that was all it took. They killed my sister and a kid we'd taken in. Dad made me go. He made me leave them, but I couldn't just go without knowing, so I came back a few hours later. Eyes front so we don't get killed out here."

"Eyes front? Play a lot of video games?"

"I'm in the Army, dumbass. I was home on leave when this shit went down."

"Would you two kindly shut the fuck up?" Joel whispered.

We'd covered a few blocks when Joel stuck his hand up, fist closed. I stopped and fought my twisted foot. We were in the backyard of a house with a dead lawn and a small fence. I staggered to the fence and lowered myself to my knees, then covered Joel as he advanced on the house. He paused in the middle of the yard and didn't move for a few seconds, then ran toward the side of the house and planted himself in a deep shadow.

The back of the home had a shattered sliding glass door; the accompanying screen door was in shreds on the ground. There was a body sticking its legs out of the doorway. They didn't move.

Noises near the street in front of the home.

Roz turned her gun to the side and examined it, then slid a few shells into the breech. Then there was movement out front; Joel faded from sight, but he wasn't gone long. Like someone had set his ass on fire, he came running back.

"Thirty or forty of them on my three o'clock."

"We're cut off?"

"Worse, there's lights in Fortress. We're blown."

I swore like the sailor I am for a few seconds.

"Back to my house. We have supplies and it used to be boarded up before Dad got himself killed," Roz said.

"The house we just left? Could have told us that before we walked half the fucking city," Joel said we moved around a fence keeping low.

"You asked for my help, man. You didn't ask me for a place to stay, so secure that fucking attitude."

"Well, yes ma'am," Joel said. I could almost hear his eye-roll.

"It's safe for the night, then we can try your place again."

"No reason to go back there. It'll be picked clean." Joel said.

I wanted to punch someone.

"I don't think we have a choice," I said between clenched teeth.

Something shambled near us in the dark. I glanced up, almost too late.

A figure stumbled upon us, moaning, white eyes searching. Its mouth was stretched into a jagged grin of glee. Joel didn't hesitate. He shot the fucker, but missed a head-shot in his haste. The shot nicked its throat, though, and spun it to the side. I hopped up on my bad foot and almost screamed in pain. I covered by swinging the wrench into the Z's jaw. The blow arced upward as I stood, so it had the force of a fucking car wreck and lifted the Z off the ground. It flopped backward and didn't move.

Joel shot another shape and then Roz fired her shotgun, blowing a hole in the middle of a Z.

"Shit! Zulu's everywhere! Go go go!" Joel said, and we did just that.

We hauled ass, Joel weaving between fences and houses as we tried to keep up. My twisted foot was a constant shriek of pain, but it was better than the alternative.

We broke through a bunch of dried up shrubs and were on the other side of the house we'd just left. Roz tapped Joel and pointed at a single story home right next to it. The place was darker than fortress and as we drew closer I realized why. Boards had been nailed to the inside of the windows. The door was shut but writing was spray-painted onto it.

"Looters will be shot by well-armed occupants."

Well, hell. That had been our trick at Fortress. I guess advertising wasn't such a good idea. Someone must have waited for us to leave and then moved in on our territory. Voices. Now I knew I'd heard them. Now they were in our home. I had a brief fantasy of Joel using his assault rifle with some kind of scope that can see through walls to take out the sons of bitches.

We moved into the open, but a shaped drifted near the front of the house and then stopped to stare at the moon. The figure swayed back and forth. Joel lifted his AR but I waved him off.

Another shape came into view and stood next to the first. The man wore a ripped t-shirt and nothing else. His legs hung with grey slack skin. The girl wore what was once a white dress. She was tiny and one arm flopped against her side when she lurched.

I lifted my wrench and pointed. Roz got the idea and produced a huge knife with a serrated edge.

I leaned over and whispered to Joel, "Cover us."

Joel nodded, pointed, and drew his finger across his neck. He then put his finger to his lip and blew gently.

Roz headed straight toward the man, leaving me the girl. I would have cut Roz off but I couldn't walk fast enough. I 'hmphed' and advanced with her.

We were a few feet away when the guy turned. Roz had the knife raised and was about to drive it into his skull. The girl didn't see me, so when the man surprised us I changed tactics and hit him across the head. Roz turned on me and I thought she was going to drive the knife into me.

The guy fell to the side but his foot spasmodically kicked out and tangled with Roz's legs. They both went down, and the girl in the white dress, seeing her opportunity, leaped on top of Roz. Roz pushed her up by the neck, but when I swung, the girl rolled to the side and my blow sailed over both of them. The girl snarled as she tried to get back on top of Roz, but Roz was having none of that. She came up in a crouch and drove the blade into the girl's chest.

Blood gushed from the Z's mouth. The knife got stuck, so I leaned over, aiming carefully this time, and crushed the girl's head with the wrench.

Together we staggered into the house and Roz quietly closed the door behind us. There was a thick metal bar in the hallway. She and Joel picked it up and dropped it into slots on either side of the entry way. Then she showed us a huge dresser that she and Joel pushed against the door.

Roz held up a hand, so we waited. She marched down the hallway and looked into rooms. She came back and moved into the kitchen and then the living room, training the shotgun on every corner. She finally came back and ushered us in.

We staggered into what had been the living room and Roz collapsed on a couch.

"Don't you ever fucking do that to me again, asshole," she said.

I looked around in confusion. Me?

"What?"

"I had that shit, man. You didn't have to get in my way."

"Yeah, Creed. Fucking jerk," Joel added from a dark corner.

"I'm going to bed. You fuckers try anything and I got a shotgun shell with your name on it."

The room was too dark to show Roz clearly, but I couldn't help noticing that she had a knockout figure.

"We aren't animals," Joel said.

"Whatever, man. Just keep your dicks out here and no one gets killed."

A door closed down the hallway.

We were left in a strange place and it was pitch black. Joel slipped on his NVG's and moved around the house.

I laid back on a lazy-boy, propped my feet up, and tried not to think of how miserable I felt. Damn leg hurt. I was thirsty, fucking exhausted, and so hungry I could eat about six meals.

After some rustling around, Joel came back and put something in my lap. I almost broke into tears when I realized it was bottled water and a pair of food bars in plastic wrappers.

It's late and I can't write any more. It was hard enough getting used to sleeping in Fortress; now we have this temporary home around us and a new friend.

This is Machinist Mate First Class Jackson Creed and I am still alive.

THE BASE

9:15 hours approximate
Location: San Diego CA – Roz's Place

After losing Fortress last night, we crashed with our new friend Roz. She's about five-foot-five and Latino. She's got dark brown hair and she'd probably clean up pretty nice. Roz is cute, I won't lie, and she's got some killer bod, at least the little I noticed while I had my arm draped over her shoulder last night. She also looks like she will kill me if I look at her that way again.

My leg is a mess. I hurt my ankle last night and now it's swollen, but I don't think it's a full sprain. I can walk on it, even though it's more of a hobble than an actual steady stride. Joel Kelly just looked at me like I was a puss. Fuck you, Marine-boy. I did it protecting you and Roz.

Roz tossed me an ace bandage so I could wrap it tight. I wish I had ice. I also wish a Burger King drive-through worked by hot strippers would suddenly appear where the front window is boarded up. I wish I had a way to go back in time a few years and tell Jenny Collins that I liked her. Not love, just liked. We did some shit over her clothes, but I know I could have gotten her with a little more skill. Might as well wish for a tropical get-away while I'm at it.

Joel was nothing but unhappy smiles and pissy Marine attitude. He stormed around all morning. Stripped his gun, put it back together, counted rounds, swore a lot, and snapped at either one of us if we asked him what the plan was.

I asked about eight times.

We had water and food, but mostly some kind of emergency rations Roz's father had collected over the last couple of years. They'd started the end of the world out with a three-month supply of food and clean drinking water for four, but after inviting in a few family members and a kid from the neighborhood, they'd used up a decent chunk. We drank sparingly, but it was hard not to guzzle. The last time I had clean water was about a week ago.

Joel finally got cabin fever and said he was going to check on Fortress.

"I'll go with you."

"Rest your foot. We may need to get mobile soon. I'll be right back."

"Dude. I'll go. You can't make it without me."

"Believe it or not, I'm a Marine and I don't need a gimp squid tagging along, asking me to wipe his nose."

"Whatever. If you run into trouble what are you going to do?"

"At the first sign of a real threat I'll come back. Get some sleep and don't give Roz any shit."

Like I wanted a knife in my chest.

"Your idea of trouble and my idea are different. You think a pack of Z's is a challenge. I think they're a death squad."

"Whatever. Just chill. I'll be back. Here – write about Reynolds, because he deserves it." Joel dropped the log book in my lap.

He'd already strapped on his combat gear and filled his pouches with magazines and a couple of energy bars from Roz's stash. He downed a bottle of water in three gulps and slid the blinds aside to take a look.

Shit. That was one day I wanted to erase from my memory. But he had a point. If we were to honor Reynolds' sacrifice, it needed to start with his story. I can't say that his story will ever be more important than those of the millions that have already died, but to us, he was a hero. The kind you hear about on the nightly news.

Jesus. The media, TV, newspapers, and cell towers. None of that shit works anymore. None of it. And that is just the start of the hell we now live in.

Joel shot me the finger and then closed the front door quietly behind him.

08:15 hours approximate
Location: A little yellow life raft, San Diego CA

Weapons:

- 1 Colt 1911 .45
- 22 Rounds of .45 ammo
- 1 Heckler and Koch MP5-N sub machine gun
- 14 Rounds 9X19 Parabellum
- 1 large knife

Near distance - a massive fire. Gunships. Jets rocketing overhead. Explosions. Fire. Smoke and chaos.

Ahead was the biggest disaster—the USS McClusky. My home for the last year. She crashed into the pier at close to full speed and that was all she wrote. But that wasn't the only thing burning. The rest of the base was a crazy mess of flames, smoke, and gunfire. Even from this distance, we heard the guns, and they were not being kind to whoever they were aimed at.

A haze settled in as the morning sun rose, further obscuring our view of the naval base. The view snapped quickly back, however, thanks to a plane that roared close to the surface of the water.

"The fuck was that?" I yelled over the noise.

"That was an A-10 warthog. They fly low and blow up tanks and stuff."

"Do you think the same shit that went down on the ship is happening there?" Reynolds pointed.

"It's some shit. That's for sure," Kelly said.

The Marines went over their gear as we closed in. We had to angle around the piers because there didn't appear to be a way to climb up. A ship rides up about twenty feet in the air, so that means the piers are a long way up and I wasn't sure we'd be able to Bruce Willis our asses up some rope.

Luckily, a smaller pier cut to the south of us, so we followed land until we could angle in. Planes continued to rocket over head. To my horror, the fuckers were shooting at people on the ground. Machine guns rattled and spent munitions fell.

"Fucking hell!" Reynolds said exactly what I was thinking.

Another jet started firing from directly overhead. A building bloomed into flame in the distance and then an explosion from another section of the base roared into the air.

"Jesus! Are we at war?" Reynolds was once again thinking my thoughts.

"I don't know. Should we even try to make it to land? Maybe we can paddle toward the city," I said.

"It's the base. We gotta help." Kelly made a lot of sense – unfortunately.

A couple of helicopters shook the raft as they flew by. They settled over the eastern part of the base and opened fire on something. More flames rose into the air. The shots weren't confined to just the aircraft. From the distance we picked up on plenty of small arms fire.

"It's the same stuff from the boat. The same goddamn stuff but its spread all over the base," Reynolds said.

"What if it's more widespread than just the base? What then?" I felt like I was whining but Kelly got a faraway look in his eye.

We came alongside a small tender and I used the railing to pull us along until we were flush with a pier. Reynolds crawled over first with his MP-5 pointing ahead. Kelly covered him and then I was next. I didn't have a weapon but I spotted a large toolbox near a small ship and lifted the lid. Inside were a number of screw drivers, nuts, bolts, and assorted tools, but the prize was a pipe wrench nearly two feet long. I lifted it and found the heft to my liking.

Kelly shot me a questioning look so I mimed bashing in a head.

"Too heavy."

"Maybe for you, ya scrawny Marine," I said.

He smirked and nodded toward Reynolds, who was taking up position next to a building with corrugated metal siding. I was surprised they hadn't left my sorry ass yet. I didn't have a fancy gun and hadn't fired one in years with the exception of video games. In virtual life I'd probably killed an entire nation of people; in real life I had no desire to shoot at another person for as long as I lived.

I followed because I didn't know what else to do. I knew the base, which meant I knew where the commissary and bars were. I knew how to get off the base for the same reason. Food, beer, and occasionally to find a date, even if it had to be paid for in Tijuana.

I could always desert these guys and just find the barracks I'd stayed in a few times, but what if that was also under attack? What a clusterfuck my day was turning into.

Gunfire to the west drew my attention. I snapped my wrench up like I was going to bat bullets out to the air. Reynolds had extended the stock of the little machine gun and moved ahead of us in a quick, steady manner. He slipped to the side of a building, slid along it to a corner and then peeked around. He motioned and Kelly followed while I brought up the rear.

Something roared nearby, causing me to spin in fear. I hit the side of the metal building with the wrench and immediately regretted it. The sound was like a Chinese game-show gong in the morning air.

A column of smoke rose from the direction of the noise that has startled me, and then an unholy explosion shook the ground. A building went up in flames, the roof disintegrating as it exploded.

A HUMVEE overflowing with people zipped past us. A guy hung onto the roof while someone else batted at the figure from the hatch. Then it was gone, careening behind another building. It grew silent for a few seconds before the vehicle crashed.

"Let's check it out," Joel said.

"Let's not and say we did," I muttered. "Fuck this, dude. We need to find someone in charge and report in. We have to tell them about the McClusky."

"I hear ya, but something is going on. Something bad. Caution is what we need right now," Reynolds said.

"And that caution means investigating crashed HUMVEES? That's what just passed, right?" I asked.

"It was, and it had Marine insignia, so it's our duty."

"Oh Christ. At least give me a gun."

"As soon as I have a spare," Joel Kelly said and clapped me on the shoulder.

Joel nodded and moved toward the sound of the crash with his handgun ready. Reynolds moved behind me and covered us as I followed the Marine.

Then someone staggered around the side of the building, but stopped when he saw us. The guy was dressed in BDU's. His head, face, and mustache were all covered in blood. It dribbled from a wound on his forehead that wasn't going to stop bleeding anytime soon, unless he put a bandage on it.

"Damn, man," I said. "You okay?"

"I don't think he's okay," Reynolds said.

Joel grabbed my shirtsleeve and shook his head.

"But he looks hurt and he's a squid—so there. You guys and your 'always going back for your own'."

"Dude ain't normal. Look at him," Reynolds said.

He was right.

The sailor advanced on us with an unsteady walk, like he was drunk off his ass. He snarled and moaned as he stumbled over his own two feet. One arm came up and that's when I noticed that his other arm was hanging at a weird angle. Not only that, but some of his fingers were completely gone.

"Is he like one of the guys on the ship?"

"Looks like it," Reynolds said.

"Sir. Sir!" Joel yelled and advanced.

Goddamn Marine. I moved ahead to block his aim because I wasn't going to watch him gun down another squid. If this guy was in shock from the accident, I didn't want these trigger-happy gun jocks shooting him just because he couldn't walk right.

Then the sailor attacked me.

I batted his arms aside and wished to hell I'd never gotten in Joel's way. The blood-splattered guy was crazy and he reeked of shit! He grabbed for me, but his hands didn't have enough fingers to get a hold on my shirt. He swung his other arm like a club and caught me across the temple. I briefly saw stars, but I'd been hit harder by one of my brothers and brushed it off.

I pushed him back but he swung his arms up again and opened his trap. Oh, fuck me, but that was some horror. His mouth was filled with broken teeth and blood. His tongue dangled out on a strip of muscle and flopped against his chin. He snarled and groaned but couldn't get his tongue back in. It would have been funny as shit if he hadn't been attempting to eat me.

I staggered backward and almost fell, but Joel really did have my back.

Joel used his body to keep me from falling and then pushed me off. That was all I needed.

I swung because I was scared. Of course, at that point I'd only seen the things on the ship and they'd frightened me, but I was also in denial, like the whole event wasn't really happening. Yet here was another of the crazy things and he wanted to kill me, not talk.

He drooled red saliva. When he tried to snarl again, blood bubbled out and something pink fell out of his mouth. It smacked the ground and I was left to stare at a piece of partially chewed human skin.

That's when I lost it. I swung the wrench with a cry and hit the bastard across the side of his head. The tool weighed about eight pounds, so it was practically a battering ram.

He dropped and didn't move again.

"Nice work," Joel said.

I wanted to puke. I'll never forget that sound, man. I'll never forget what it felt like to hit a human like that. I was horrified and I was disgusted.

More gunfire all around us and then another series of jets roared overhead. I ducked but looked up as they departed. A few seconds later, the sounds of explosions reverberated in the direction of the city.

Joel looked troubled, gestured for me to follow, and moved out.

They were hitting the city? Good Christ, how far had this spread?

We came across the crash a few minutes later. The Humvee had struck the side of a building filled with ship parts. Whoever had been on top of the military truck was smashed against the wall in a smear of blood and gore that would haunt my nightmares for days to come. Shit! This whole damn day was going to necessitate a hell of a lot of therapy.

A soldier rolled out of a rear door and fell onto the ground. He didn't move for a few seconds. We stared at each other and then back at him. From the angle he lay in, it seemed obvious that his hips had to be broken. Legs just couldn't be in that position. He twitched and I was afraid he was one of them, but he got one hand under his body and lifted himself up a few inches so he could look at us. Joel moved in, gun trained on the guy.

"Help," the man said. He was dressed in camo and had a host of magazines and bulging pockets on his upper body.

"Damn. What happened, brother?" Joel moved in and helped the guy roll over.

"Everything. I'm hurt bad. Can you get someone to help? Please? Take me to medical or get a chopper."

"Hold on. We'll do our best. I promise," Reynolds said. He dropped beside Joel Kelly and me and took the hurt man's hand in his.

Blood spread across the fallen Marine's tactical vest. Reynolds leaned over and opened it to reveal that something had penetrated his chest. He took a gurgling breath and then sighed.

"This is not good," Reynolds said.

"It's bad, man. I can't even feel my legs."

"Help's on the way," Joel said.

Was it? I didn't hear the sound of sirens or see the flash of red lights.

"It's worse than that. Ah, shit. Just gimme a gun and one shot, then go. Get the fuck out of here and don't look back."

That's when I saw it. The sleeve of his other arm was ripped open and blood, fresh and crimson, coated the fabric. He'd removed his belt and cinched it just below his elbow. The man had been bitten, and assuming that what had happened on the ship was "the new normal," this guy was so screwed.

"What happened?"

"It's all messed up. So royally messed up. Were you here when it started?"

"No brother. We were on a ship. Just got here."

"Shit. Lucky you. It's a virus of some kind. Whole city's gone crazy. We heard the same stuff hit other bases."

"What's your name?"

"Norvell, Mike Norvell. Guys used to call me Big Papa." Mike choked on a glob of blood and spat it out.

"Tell me about the base, Norvell."

"You guys need to go," Norvell gasped and then frowned. His body stiffened and he looked about as miserable as anyone I'd ever seen in my life.

"You're going to be alright."

"The tourniquet slows it down but I can feel it. It's like my blood's filled with sand."

"Sorry we can't do better by you, man. But please. What happened?"

"It happened so fast. Something docked that wasn't supposed to, some ship from overseas. They quarantined it, but something happened. A few days later the first cases showed up. Then rumors. Rumors of the virus at other seaports and military bases."

"What? Like an attack?"

I unholstered the gun at Norvell's side, held it up and ejected the magazine. I took out all but one bullet, pocketed what I was pretty sure were 9 mm rounds, put the magazine back in and racked a shell into the chamber. I held the gun out to Reynolds. He took it, stared at it for a few seconds and then put it in the guy's hand.

Norvell coughed up another blast of blood and that seemed to be enough for Reynolds. The Marine got to his feet and moved back. Mike "Big Papa" Norvell thrashed on the ground. His eyes bulged so much I thought they were going to explode. He shook as he lifted his hand and just barely managed to put the barrel of the gun under his chin.

We all looked away when the shot snapped across the area.

Joel got up and went to the vehicle. He rummaged around and then came out with a rifle and a small backpack. He put the items on the ground and hunted around again. He came out with a pair of handguns, then placed four magazines on the ground.

Joel had a crap load of gear laid out. The guys, still soaking wet from the dip in the ocean, strapped on as much as they could, to a soundtrack of squishing noises. Reynolds slung his little machine gun behind his back, picked up one of the rifles and checked it. They tossed me a handgun. I did as I'd done with Norvell's gun because I wasn't a complete idiot when it came to weapons. I did a quick inspection, counted how many rounds I had in the Smith and Wesson, then added a pair of magazines to my pockets.

We moved out toward the center of base. Why? I had no idea; I was just along for the walk in hell. Before we departed, Joel looked over the HUMVEE just to make sure it was toast. Didn't take a fucking mechanic to see the damage was beyond any of us or a shop, a week, and a hell of a repair bill. The front end was completely destroyed from hitting the corner of the building, but the seats were also covered in blood, and that was reason enough for me to stay out.

Two buildings later, we ran into a shit storm.

Someone had set up a barricade of cars, trucks, and fences to block at least one cross-street. Joel jogged the perimeter and then dashed back a minute later. He shook his head, so we looked back the way we'd come.

Joel was in the process of hauling ass around the corner of a barracks when he ran smack into one of the creatures. It was missing part of a foot and toppled over when Joel struck him. The Marine didn't hesitate; he splattered its brains all over the road with two quick shots.

"Oh, fuck me running!" Reynolds said.

I echoed his sentiment in my head.

There had to be fifty of them massed around the remains of the barricade. Bodies were pressing against the corners and they weren't interested in the fence, because they were eating – Fucking eating – the soldiers.

"Oh no you don't!" Reynolds yelled.

He started shooting. The booming of his assault rifle was ridiculously loud. Joel Kelly took a wide stance and also started popping guys in the head, neck, and body. He practically ripped a guy's arm off with a couple of shots, then a beauty of a blast took the guy right through the temple as he tried to turn on us.

I raised my own gun to take aim, and then I couldn't pull the trigger. The uniformed person that fell under my aim was a woman about my age. She was slight and had a head of blonde hair. I would have given her a second and third look if we passed each other on the street.

Now she was covered in her own blood—or someone else's. Her shirt was ripped away, revealing lots of pale flesh, but I was not interested in the slightest. One of her breasts was practically torn away. Talk about the opposite of a little blue pill.

I turned to gag. Kelly, seeing me in distress, shot her twice. The first shot was off to her shoulder but he snapped the gun up and put one through her nose. She collapsed without a sound.

"Fuck this!" That was it for me. I shuddered in revulsion and considered jumping back into the ocean.

"Get it together, man!" Joel Kelly said, and I thought he was going to hit me.

Reynolds stayed in the fight and fired as quickly as he could focus in on targets. Joel moved to assist, so I decided it was time to man the fuck up.

I put an advancing soldier that slobbered and drooled blood between my cross hairs and shot him three times. The first two went to his chest; those just backed him up. I knew how this shit worked, so I shot him in the head as my brain caught up with the rest of my body.

Then a tide of them came at us. It was like the flood gates had opened. Holy shit, there were a lot of the undead bastards. They poured out of buildings, side roads, out of stopped vehicles, and

God knew where else. I said a prayer, but Joel had a better idea.

"Fall back. Let's head for the barracks."

Reynolds followed him but I took a few seconds to shoot the lead Z a couple of times, and then my gun ran empty. I pulled the trigger on the Smith and Wesson but it just clicked. Kelly was the one to break me out of my daze by smacking me upside the head.

"Don't touch me!" I screamed.

"Get your head in the game, man. Let's go!"

He was right. There were ten or fifteen of them for each one of us and more coming. The only thing stopping them from overrunning our position were the remains of the barricade. We could make a valiant stand and take a shit load of them with us.

Or we could do something else. We could haul ass.

We did the latter.

12:25 hours approximate
Location: San Diego CA – Roz's Place

It's been a week since that day, and I still think about it maybe more than everything else that's happened since. But I'll have to get to that later.

Joel's back from his little trip to Fortress and he isn't alone. He brought a couple of teenagers with him. Were these the little shits that broke into our house?

Joel had knocked on the door three times and then once. He'd paused and done it again, so Roz opened the door. She took one look at him and at the two dirty faced behind him, and she didn't seem annoyed or put out at all. She just motioned for them to come inside.

Roz took one look at them and motioned for them to join us.

"Fortress?" I asked.

"Gone, but we got bigger problems."

"Bigger? What's bigger than losing our home?"

"Losing everything. That's a hell of a lot bigger."

"What do you mean?"

Joel turned to the kids – a boy and girl – and nodded. The girl was fifteen at the most. She tried to look brave but she was a mess. Her hair was a pale bird's nest that pointed in every direction. The boy was older by a few years and he was well armed. He had a small bat slung over his back. The strap was a piece of rope but I noticed right away it would be easy to swing it under his arm and have it at the ready.

He had a pair of knives tucked into his belt and a snub nose revolver in a holster at his waist. Call this kid Dirty Harry.

"I'm Christie and this is Craig."

"Hey." Craig nodded.

He had a deep voice for such a skinny kid. If he weighed a buck ten I'd be surprised. But he was gangly and I bet he could swing that little baseball bat with devastating force. They were both dressed in clothes that had seen better days a week ago.

Now they were practically rags and covered in dirt. Neither one smelled all that great, but who was I to judge? Joel and I had lived in our own sweat for ten or eleven days now.

"So you took over our home?"

"Wasn't us. Someone came before and searched it. We just moved in after they left. Thought you guys were gone."

"Was that you I heard rummaging around the night before?"

"Yeah. Sorry about that. We were so hungry but we waited until you were gone. We were just going to eat some food and leave, but the other guys got there first. Not us. We went in later. Got a few scraps."

Roz went to the kitchen and cracked open some packages. She brought them both bottled water and a "meal ready to eat" apiece. They tore into it like it was a number 3 at McDonalds.

"So who took our shit?"

"Some dudes that looked like they were ready for war. Looked tougher than you guys."

Joel burst into laughter.

"We do alright," I protested.

Craig looked us over but clearly wasn't impressed.

I stared at the kid for a minute while that processed. A helicopter overhead rattled the windows, giving me a scare and a half.

Joel moved to the window and cracked open the blinds to look up. He craned his neck around but shook his head after a few seconds.

"We're saved?" I asked Joel.

"Can't tell, man, but it can't be worse than a city full of fucking zombies."

Roz 'hmphed' and looked toward the kids.

"Sorry. Gosh darned zombies."

Both of the young ones snickered.

"What else could it be?" I asked.

The answer to that question would come soon because Joel was gearing up, and that meant we were going to reconnoiter. I thought about my swollen ankle and decided that if he was going out, I was going along as well. Enough of this sitting around.

I'd have to wrap it tight and take my chances, because I was not letting the Marine go out there without me. I'll finish up the story of how we got off the base and founded Fortress later.

This is Machinist Mate First Class Jackson Creed and I am still alive.

FIGHT AND FLIGHT

19:45 hours approximate
Location: San Diego CA – Roz's Roof

Supplies:

- Food: a few protein bars
- Weapons: almost zip

Worst. Day. Ever.

My dad was a big guy who didn't talk much. He was in the Army and told me that the military wasn't the best place for a kid like me. He said I'd be better suited for a blue-collar job like construction or sanitation where I didn't have someone constantly telling me when to wipe my ass. I said that would be funny if I was in sanitation. He smacked me upside the head.

Why didn't I listen to him? He was a goddamn genius.

Don't get me wrong, I got nothing against blue-collar workers or the job I ended up with in the Navy. Someone's gotta keep the fires on a ship lit. Gotta keep that engine turning. I just wanted to do something different, like get into journalism, but that required money. I joined the Navy so I could see the world, fuck a lot of girls, and then have my college paid for.

I got one of those wishes.

One wish I didn't make was for my very own Marine Sergeant Joel "Cruze" Kelly. One night I asked Joel what the "Cruze" was all about. He smiled and deflected the question. Jerk. I kept bugging him about it, because what the hell else did we have to talk about? I asked if it was some kind of Marine secret handshake. After a few minutes of my good-natured ribbing, he finally told me it was something his Mom had called him as a kid and it just stuck around. I didn't bother him about it after that.

My own mother didn't have an opinion either way about me joining up. On one hand, I'm sure she didn't want her youngest son leaving the house. On the other hand, it was probably a relief. My three older bothers weren't amounting to much and continued to mooch off our folks while I had dreams of going to college. Money I wasn't going to make working at Burger King.

I was going to join the Army, like Dad, but then I watched some videos of boot camp and decided a ship would be a much more interesting place to hang out instead of in the sand while some asshole shot at me.

Joel did not have a similar story. His dad was in the Marines, and his dad's dad was in the Corps, so that meant that Joel Kelly was destined to hold an assault rifle and shoot at people. Hoo-ah – oh yeah, they don't say that in the Marines anymore. If Joel reminded me of that one more time I was going to strangle him with his own gun strap.

Roz didn't tell us much more of her story but she listened to us talk about our pasts and asked questions when it seemed like there was a break in the flow. She said it would be a way for all of us to break the ice and get to know each other. Now that we had a couple of kids with us, I guess it made sense.

I know it sounds like I'm planning for the future, but I'm not really. When you get right down to it, our life expectancy is next to nil. When you really think about what we are facing, you'll understand that it's not a good idea to make long term plans.

Especially now.

Especially. Now!

15:45 hours approximate
Location: San Diego CA – Roz's Place

Joel snoozed in my chair for an hour. I took the time to eat and drink as much as my gut could handle.

It was glorious.

Roz was busy pacing the living room. She walked to the front door and then back to the windows that faced the yard. I took the opportunity to check out her ass in a pair of grey sweat pants that seemed molded to her body. I'm glad she didn't catch me. I'm pretty sure she'd have no issue with sticking her shotgun up my ass. Roz peeked out every few minutes. After a while she must have made up her mind to do whatever she needed to do, because she woke Joel up and asked for cover.

Joel popped up like a Marine Jack-in-the-Box, snapped up his assault rifle, and did a quick ammo check. He nodded at Roz and followed her to the door.

"What's she doing?" I asked Joel.

"Her father."

"Oh," I said, and lost whatever little bit of a good mood I'd had a few minutes ago. No kid should have to bury their own parent.

"Should I help?"

"I don't think so. She looks determined to do it herself. Why don't you keep watch out the back."

Roz went into the open garage and dragged out an old carpet. She took the piece to her Dad's body and rolled him onto it. Smart. That way she could drag him easier, and it also created a sort of burial cover.

I went to the back of the house and peeked through a window. This was Roz's room and we'd been forbidden from entering it. I had a feeling she wouldn't mind since we were protecting her.

She wasn't the neatest girl. There were clothes in piles all around the room. Shirts and dresses hung from a homemade wire rack that ran the length of the room. Dresses? That was the last thing I expected to see Roz in. After a few minutes it hit me. What else was she supposed to do with her clothes? There sure as hell wasn't any way to wash them in our new world.

The back room's windows were boarded up but a couple of spy holes offered me a limited view of the world outside the house. Dried up shrubs, a road littered with discarded crap. Broken furniture and empty suitcases. Someone's sports jacket baked in the sun next to a pair of white broken white sunglasses. The only things missing were a few shamblers.

In salute to the dead world I lifted a plastic wrapper, tore it open, and munched on a protein bar. Then I sipped a bottle of water. The only thing that would make this better was an ice-cold beer, but the lone brew we'd saved from our beer-run a few days ago was probably in the coffers of whoever the fuck ransacked our place.

It was early but already hot inside the little brick house. It may be seventy five at the hottest out there, but once the place gets warm it stays that way.

Sound to the west. I was on the east-facing side of the house and couldn't see a damn thing until the helicopter thundered overhead. It hovered for a few seconds over a building and then passed over the house. Did they see Roz? Did she signal to them? Were they going to come back and rescue us?

Over a week in this city and I was sick of being cut off. I was sick of living day to day, meal to meal. I wanted out of San Diego and I wanted to know, more than anything, what in the hell was happening in the good ol' U S of A, because the way we were living could not be the new normal.

I pulled my handgun before I'd even had the chance to think about it. If I could just signal the chopper

I popped the magazine out of habit and checked the load. Full. I lined it up and then fumble fingered the mag. It hit the ground and bounced under Roz's bed. I followed it and dropped to all fours to get it. I got a handful of panties and stockings and stared at them dumbly. I bet Roz would rock this stuff.

I carefully put the naughty clothes back, picked up the heavy magazine, and slammed it home.

The sound of the chopper was long gone. I stared up but they didn't materialize again. Then I looked down.

"Oh. Fuck. Me." I holstered my pistol.

A horde was headed our way. I don't mean ten Z's or fifty of the dead fuckers. It was even worse than the day we almost got stuck in Ty's apartment when Joel's little fuck up seemed to bring the whole city our way. Only speed and luck had saved our ass that time.

There had to be several thousands. Thousands!

"Uhh," I said. Real smart, right?

I was so scared I considered just crapping my pants. Then Joel's voice in my head told me to man up or he'd find an adult diaper and make me wear it. Here we were in a nice safe house where we could silently wait for them to pass us by, and Roz was out on the front yard. There wasn't even a moment of hesitation, no thought of leaving her out there.

I stared and tried to get a count but after a few seconds I dashed out of the room.

I ran at a gimpy pace on my twisted ankle through the hallway. I passed a room where the two kids, Christy and Craig, slept. I made it to the living room and almost crashed into the recliner I'd called home the night before.

"Joel!" I called as loudly as I dared.

He had the door propped open, one foot inside the threshold, the other on the porch. The assault rifle was slung across his chest with his finger poised right over the trigger. Joel wore his New York Fire Department ball cap backwards and the pilfered shades over his eyes.

"Joel!" I yelled louder this time.

"What? I'm keeping watch. Why aren't you doing the same?"

"Dude. We got trouble. Big fucking trouble."

"What?"

"Come look."

"I can't leave Roz out there."

"Roz. Shit."

I didn't have to think about the stupid shit I was about to do.

I tried to brush past Joel but he stopped me with a meaty Marine hand. I towered over him and could have knocked him aside, but for all the shit we give each other, I'd never had a better friend.

"What're you doing?"

"It's bad. There're so many of them I couldn't count the first wave. It's an army and they're all headed in this direction. We need to get Roz back in here now." I looked around the yard. "Where is she?"

"In the garage. Please tell me you're exaggerating a little bit."

"I wish, man. I wish. Did she flag down that chopper?"

"They took off when they saw her."

"Damn."

"You go get her. I'll cover. No, wait. You cover and I'll go. You and your busted leg."

"You're ten times the shot I am. I'll go." And this time I did take his hand, but with more of a handshake grip as I pushed it down. "It's the right thing to do. Stay here and pop anything that gets close."

Joel nodded and clapped me on the shoulder.

I did the stupid thing and took a step outside the house.

#

16:05 hours approximate
Location: San Diego CA – Roz's Place

The garage wasn't attached to the house. If it was, this might have had a different ending. As it was, the little building was only thirty or forty feet away from the door and only a few feet from the side of the house, but it might as well have been a mile with me naked and armed with a toothbrush.

I swear I could hear them already, even though they had to be at least a hundred yards away.

The morning sun was nice and high in the sky. I shaded my eyes and crunched across the short concrete patio, down the couple of stairs, and onto the sidewalk. Dead grass in all of its yellow and brown glory spread around me. A lone water sprinkler sat next to a dried blood stain which roughly resembled the shape of a man.

The corner of the house erupted in noise. The moans of the dead had reached us much quicker than I thought and that meant one thing.

Shufflers.

A group came into view from the side of the garage. They were a motley assortment of dead, cobbled together by their need for fresh meat. Men and women, boys and girls. The virus had taken everyone in its path.

"Ugly bastards, all of you!" I yelled.

I hoped Roz heard me. I was already headed toward her, so I drew and shot on the move. I missed. My second shot missed as well, so I stopped, took a breath, aimed down the sights and then dropped the Z that was about to enter the garage.

I spun but more of the Z's were rounding the other side of the house. I was trapped.

Hobbling on my bum ankle, I got to the walkway. Joel swung into his super Marine mode by moving onto the porch and dropping the first of the dead. His second shot spun another one around but it completed a halfway decent dance move by turning three hundred and sixty degrees. Joel hit it between the eyes with the second shot.

Another pair right behind the first. I gasped and took a shot. Missed. God I sucked. My hand was shaking like a leaf but I didn't stop firing.

A couple of former soldiers, from the look of their rotted and hanging uniforms. I took out one and hit the other in the chest. He dropped but got a hand out and hauled himself to his knees. I kicked the rotter in the face and dove into the garage.

The bodies from the night before lay in a pile. Roz had executed one at point blank range and most of his head was just gone. Joel's shots had been neater but the bodies were still that—bodies.

"Oh no! Oh shit!" Roz yelled.

"Can you close the door?"

"Shit!" She jumped and grabbed a rope and yanked but the door didn't budge.

The former soldier I'd kicked in the face snarled around a dislocated jaw and came at us. I kicked him in the gut before he could reach the boundary of the garage. He was dead, so he needed to stay on his side of the world. I used the best persuader at my disposal by lifting the hand cannon and firing into his face.

I'd made good use of the gun, but in the heat of the battle I'd lost count of my shots. I went over the action in my head and thought I might have seven or eight rounds left.

Roz grabbed at the door again. I got a hold on the rope with her, this time, and we both yanked. The garage door came loose and slid down with a creak.

The old and heavy slab of wood swung down and dropped into place. It clicked when it was flush with the ground, so I tested the handle, but it wouldn't turn. At least we were safe for now, even if we were trapped in a giant box with no light and four or five bodies. My skin crawled, and that was before I got the first whiff of their bloating corpses.

More gunshots and then they went silent.

"What happened?" Roz asked. She stood close to me, so I reached out to touch her in the dark, just to reassure myself that she was really there. Of all the close calls, this one had been the worst. I was left gasping for air.

"I slipped."

"No, what happened just now?"

"I was in the back of the house keeping an eye out when I saw them coming. About a thousand of those things. I ran out to warn you."

"So you went out on a rescue mission? Are you stupid?"

"You're welcome."

"I didn't ask you to save me. I can take care of myself."

"Yeah, and those things would have devoured you. Where would that leave me and Joel? Inside the house, filled with guilt and your food. That's where."

"Chivalry's dead, man."

"But being a decent human being isn't. Not yet. Not with Joel Kelly and Jackson Fucking Creed on the case."

She let out a light giggle, and that was enough for me.

Roz touched my hand, took it in hers and squeezed. I squeezed back. We stood in the dark and didn't speak for long moments. My breathing was still harsh and came in ragged gasps.

Thumping on the door that grew in intensity. I'd seen this before, the second or third day in the city. The dead had trapped a poor soul in a hotel room and battered at the door and window until both broke. The screams came moments later.

Joel and I had been hidden in a convenience store across the street. The door had probably been busted off the hinges by looters. We crouched and stared at each other with wide, wild eyes. I was scared to death that at any moment one of those things was going to get wind of us.

We managed to keep quiet for a couple of hours while the dead feasted on their prize and then eventually wandered off. Funny how hiding makes you patient. A week ago I would have been going stir crazy from having nothing to do but wait. Back then I had my games and cell phone. I even had a crappy tablet I'd won in a game of spades. I could hang out and read Facebook or surf the web. Being stuck in that store while we contemplated life and death made me shut the fuck up with a quickness.

Roz and I only had one choice and it was in my right hand. Seven or eight shots were enough. I only needed two.

"We're fucked," Roz said.

"No back door?"

"Nope. Dad had this thing delivered and mounted on a concrete slab fifteen years ago. It's not even a real garage. It's just a bunch of wooden siding held together with bubblegum."

"What do you want to do?"

"I don't think making a run for it is an option, yeah?"

"Yeah. I mean no. Think we can kick out a wall?"

"Probably...but the noise."

"Yeah," I said.

Roz folded herself into me and stood there for a minute. She touched my chest and then felt to my shoulder, then down my arm. Shit, was I about to go out with a smile?

Her hand stopped at the handgun.

"How many rounds do you have?"

"Enough."

"Okay, but last resort. If they get in here, do it. Don't tell me it's coming; just do it so I'm not scared out of my pants."

"I bet you look good out of your pants," I said.

"Guess you'll never know in the dark, huh? Maybe we should be quiet. See? I'm coming up with a plan."

"That's the plan?"

"Yeah. If we're quiet, maybe they'll get bored and leave."

I didn't see that happening but I also didn't see anything wrong with holding Roz against me for a little bit longer. It'd been a long time since I held a woman and if I was about to die, I could think of worse ways to go.

Our respite was short lived. The pounding on the door picked up with gusto. I hugged Roz tighter and closed my eyes.

mumble mumble.

"What?" I asked the darkness.

"Someone's yelling."

"Joel. Who else would start making a fuss? Think he's going to go into Marine mode and lead them away?"

"I hope not," Roz said.

"Me too." I nodded in the dark. I liked Joel right where he was – alive and ready to carry on the fight.

More mumbled shouts.

The banging on the door increased and I was sure they were about to break in. The door flexed, so we took up station in front of it and pushed back. It might not stop them for long, but it was better than giving up.

More mumbles but they were overridden by the moans outside. So many voices and many of them just making guttural sounds. It didn't make any sense. I did, however, make out was the clicks and scrabbling of at least one shuffler.

Something thumped against the garage so hard I nearly jumped out of my skin. I'd like to say we were brave, but I was just about to go find a corner to shit in. If I didn't, my pants were going to be filled, and I didn't want my Mom's worst fear to be realized. She would have to bury my corpse in my dirty skivvies.

Something else thumped. I looked up because the sound had come from there. Jesus, did a shuffler make it that high? I'd seen them leap, but not that damn far. The roof was flat, but it was still a good twelve feet high.

Something smashed into the roof and this time I aimed the gun. More mumbled shouts.

"What in the hell!" Roz yelled. She reached for me and found my hand. I gave hers a squeeze and tried to act brave which was really hard to do in the pitch black.

Light crept under the garage door every time one of the Z's hit it. As the beating grew faster it looked like we were standing under a strobe light.

The door buckled and almost went down. A spring on one side gave way with a twanging pop. The Z's beat at the door even harder. I pushed back, but one hard crash almost sent me to my knees. That would be one of the shufflers.

More noise from the roof.

I tugged Roz to me. I embraced her and put her head against my chest. It wasn't really a romantic way to go out and not something I'd ever plan. If this was some Romeo and Juliet fucked up zombie movie, that's how it would end. I guess I'd just put the gun to her head and pull the trigger, then, if it didn't pass through her head and into my chest, I'd put it under my chin. The dead could feast on my corpse.

Still, I'd love to kill one more shuffler before I went down. I hated those things.

Something crashed into the roof. Something heavy enough to shake the entire building— speaking of shufflers.

Another crash and light poured in from above.

"Get your asses up here!" Joel yelled.

Something sharp smashed into the roof and tore a hole the size of a softball. He was using an entrenching tool to rip the roof an asshole. Son of a bitch, Joel. Son of a bitch.

The dead renewed their efforts to get us. The thumping was bad enough, but now Joel was offering us a way out – if there was time.

"Can you find some way to get us up there?" I asked Roz.

"What about the door?"

"Just make us a ladder. I'll hold the door." I smiled in the dim light because I knew it was probably a death sentence.

She moved away and used the light from above to gather up a few items. Now that I could see, it was clear that the garage was a veritable death trap. Tools lay on benches, and there was a chainsaw that I briefly thought of trying to use if the Z's got through the door.

A couple of mowers lay in disrepair with wheels and machine parts in buckets and bins. There was enough furniture in the room to fill a two-story house, most of it stacked against the wall.

Joel ripped up a chunk of roof and tossed it aside. He looked in and I waved, but with the dust and dark I doubted he could make us out.

"I can see you!" Roz yelled.

She worked at a pile of old wooden chairs, tossing them under the hole Joel was creating. He dug in with the small shovel and then ripped up yet another piece along with a huge pile of pink insulation.

The dead grew furious, judging by the way they pounded at the door. I pushed back, and just when I thought they were going to give it a rest, something hit the door hard enough to knock off another spring.

"Shufflers. We need to hurry!" Joel yelled.

"Then hurry."

"Get your ass up here and dig. I bet they'll let you through."

I flipped him the bird.

The door buckled and almost caved in. I put my back into it but there were fingers wriggling between the frame and the broken door. A hand poked through, so I dragged the gun up, estimated where the head was attached to the body, and put a round through the thick wood. The hand stopped feeling around and went limp.

"Almost got it!" Joel yelled and ripped up another piece of roof.

Roz climbed up onto the contraption she'd built and stood on unsteady legs as the chair wobbled, balanced on two other chairs. Was I supposed to get out on that thing?

She reached up; Joel Kelly caught her hands and pulled. Another pair of hands came down and grabbed her forearms and then she was yanked up. Craig or Christy, those two wonderful kids, had decided to help. I grinned.

My gratitude was short lived.

My skin crawled and my belly clenched when the door gave way. I pulled away and just avoided being crushed under it and about a hundred stinking dead people that wanted to eat me.

Do you know the dread? Can you imagine what their reek is like? It's hell, pure hell and those teeth... Most still have teeth, but others have snapped and cracked chompers that are the nastiest things you have ever seen outside of a pit of bloated corpses rotting in the sun.

I made it two steps, thought I felt breath on the back of my neck, then spun and shot a shuffler in mid-leap. She had both hands up, her mouth a furious grin of madness. I swear she was gibbering. A couple of fingers had been chewed to the knuckle and that was probably what saved me, because her nasty hand wasn't able to keep a grip on my arm.

My first shot missed. I took a few steps back as every fiber of my body screamed that I needed to run. I fired one more time and, this time, did some damage. The bullet ripped through her body laterally but didn't stop the damned woman.

I reached the chairs and crawled up the first level while the garage filled. I had only seconds and one mistake would be the end of me. I'd be pulled into the mass so fast that there wouldn't be time to blow my brains out.

I shot a Z in the chest because I didn't have time to get a good bead. The bullet punched into flesh and knocked it aside.

Up to the second set of chairs and then I could almost reach the roof.

The chair rocked under my feet but I dared not look down. If I did, I was sure one of them would have me.

I leapt up and the chair wobbled to the side.

Fingertips. That's all I managed to hold on with.

Joel grabbed an arm and pulled. Craig grabbed my other arm, and if not for them, I would have gone back down into the mass.

Another shuffler smashed into the chairs and I was left dangling like a side of beef.

"Fucking get me out of here!" I yelled in an unintended falsetto.

"We're trying, you fucking ox," Joel said as he strained.

Joel's face was full of worry, visible even behind his thick shades. He gasped for breath and threw his body into it. I rose into the air a few precious inches and managed to get a grip on the edge of the hole.

I pulled my legs up close to my body as something else grabbed at my boots. A hand got a hold of my pant leg and I was stretched between my rescuers and my would-be consumers.

I'm pretty sure I screamed like a little girl.

Roz leaned over and grabbed a wrist. Together, the three of them pulled me up. I kicked down and dislodged the hand on my pant leg. Another kick caught the shuffler in the head.

It gibbered as it fell away. The bitch's head was covered in wisps of hair and her eyes were sunken in like the orbs of a skeleton. Blood coated her body, but most of it was by her mouth. She struck the mob below and used them as a trampoline.

I was so sickened that I sat down with my feet dangling inside the garage, took aim, and shot her in the head. Her mouth moved and something like words came out, but they didn't mean anything. She stopped making noises when my round split her skull. Take that, you sick fuck.

"Thank you, Joel. Thank you for saving us." I reached out to offer a manly shake-thing that turned into a half-hearted hug until he pushed my hands away.

"You'd do the same for me," Joel said. "You might wish you were still down there."

"Why in the hell would I wish that?" I asked but trailed off when I saw the new horizon.

I rose on shaking legs, my body exhausted as adrenaline faded away. The sun was an unholy blaze that illuminated a fresh nightmare. All around the house there were the dead. Nothing but the dead. On and on the horde stretched, and more were on the way.

We were trapped in the middle of Undeadville with no escape.

"What do we do now?"

Joel shrugged and picked up his AR-15 and popped the magazine. He gave it a quick shake and slid it back home with a click.

"I guess we wait and hope they go away."

Below, the front door to the house gave in with a crash. Great; that was the second fortress we'd lost in two days.

Craig and Roz sat to the side to watch the Z's gather. Roz sat down and touched her fingers to her forehead, then down to her chest, and then side to side while muttering something about el Diablo.

"How'd you even get up here?"

Joel pointed at his entrenching tool and then looked at the house. They'd come out through the roof, jumped the couple of feet that separated the buildings and then gotten us out.

Christy popped out of the hole in the house a few seconds later and slung a couple of backpacks onto the roof. She took a deep breath and pulled herself up. Craig made the three-foot leap onto the home and helped her cross.

They both joined us and collapsed in a heap.

"I got what I could but they broke into the house."

"All that food and water," Roz said and shook her head.

"At least we're still alive." I tried to sound cheerful but it was cut off by the moans of the dead. A shuffler threw itself at the side of the garage and fell into the crowd below.

"Yeah. This is terrific." Joel said.

Joel had managed to make it out of the house with his assault rifle. He sat with it cradled in his arms.

The ocean of the dead stretched around us until they covered the ground in every direction.

This is Machinist Mate First Class Jackson Creed and I am still alive. For now…

Timothy W. Long

REINFORCEMENTS

04:35 hours approximate
Location: San Diego, CA

Supplies:

* Food: zip
* Weapons: almost zip

The roof. The roof. The roof is surrounded by the fucking dead. We just need a fire to make the mother....you get the idea.

I'm not much for long speeches. After a while all of the words sort of run into each other and become a drone. Joel Kelly also wasn't a fan of long speeches and beat me to it with this perfect summary: "We are so fucked."

You'd think a Marine would have a little more dignity or some words of wisdom. If John Wayne was playing the part of a Marine at Anzio and the enemy surrounded our little group of survivors, I'm sure he'd have some powerful words for the troops. Big words about glory and how it's a fighter's duty to destroy the bad guys.

Our troops just lowered their heads and hid. It wasn't hard. Since full dark we'd tried to sleep. The effort was there, but I had sand paper in my eyes from listening to the moans all night.

The house was full of dead. The garage was packed with the dead. The area around us as far as the eye could see was surrounded by the dead. So many dead it was like an ocean. They were out there in their rotted masses really stinking up the place. They groaned, moaned, and snarled. Christy lay on her side and tried to muffle them out with her hands. Craig stared back at them defiantly. That's what a kid's bravado is good for, right there. I had no such illusions.

"How did this mess happen?" Roz asked. She was covered in sweat and blood – not her own blood, but that of her dad and the Z's that had chased us into the garage. I'd shot a shuffler in mid-leap and blood had splattered liberally. It was probably the single best shot I'd made in my week in the city and no one even saw it. I should get a fucking medal for that blast. I settled for being alive.

"At least we're alive." I said. I got a whole pat on the hand for that.

"Why don't we sneak back into the house? Close the door. Lock it. Then we kill all the zombies. We'll be safe then," Christy whispered.

Girl didn't realize that we couldn't just take our chances like that. One bite was all it took.

"Will that work?" Craig asked and flipped one of the shufflers the bird.

"Not a chance." I broke the bad news. "We'd probably all die trying."

The shuffler hissed at Craig. He sniffed the air, looked at his slower moving brethren, and then put his hand in his mouth and bit off a finger.

The Z's left him alone while he chewed on his own digit.

Craig lay back down, so I did the same. Maybe if we stayed out of sight long enough the Z's would lose interest and wander away.

"Why do they do that?" Craig asked quietly.

"Why do they do what?"

"Act like they're afraid of the crawly dudes."

"The slow ones?" I asked.

"Yeah. They even act like they understand the weird ones."

"We call them shufflers."

"Shuffler? Like they deal cards?"

"No. On account of that shuffle step they use when they walk. It's like a stuttering motion they can't control. We thought they were running around on broken bones or maybe weren't fully turned or some shit."

"Watch your language around the kids," Roz warned.

"Language?" I blinked.

"Doesn't bother me, dude," Craig said.

"How old are you?" I asked.

"Seventeen."

"Probably has worse language than me."

"Dad was in the Navy," Craig said and looked away.

"I'm in the Navy too. It's cool. What did your Dad do?"

"Something with weapons systems."

"Good for him. I bet he had air conditioning." I thought of spending hours and hours in the hundred-degree engine room.

"Shh." Roz shot me a look.

I sighed and patted Craig's hand.

"Sorry, man. I hope your Dad's okay."

"Me too," he said.

I sighed and slipped my logbook out of the backpack that Christy had retrieved from the house, then dug around until I found a beat up pen.

Joel had pulled his NYFD hat over his eyes and snored gently. He was so quiet I couldn't even hear him over the moans of the dead below. How did he sleep in this living hell?

"What's that?" Craig asked me.

"The only thing keeping me sane," I said and set pen to paper to write about how we had escaped the base.

#

15:10 hours approximate
Location: Remains of San Diego Naval Base, CA

Weapons:

- 2 fully automatic assault rifles
- Enough magazines to make them count
- 1 Colt 1911 .45
- 22 Rounds of .45 ammo
- 1 Heckler and Koch MP5-N sub machine gun
- 1 large knife
- 1 vey large wrench

I've heard a lot of situations described as clusterfucks. I've used the term a number of times myself. Generally the word had a lot of meanings, but this was the best example I'd come across yet.

We'd been back on the base for a few hours and all we'd managed to do was run, hide, and shoot a bunch of people that were acting crazed. I know now it was the damn virus that caused the zombie apocalypse but I didn't know it then. If I'd had any clue, I might have done the smart thing and jumped back into the ocean, then would've swam until my legs gave out. With any luck, a killer whale would choke on my sorry white ass.

We'd just run from a barricade that covered multiple streets. There were dead all over the fucking place and it seemed like every one of them had a bead on us. Joel Kelly moved out on point while Reynolds brought up the rear. I stayed in the middle and tried not to trip on anything. Joel used fancy hand signals; after a while, I thought I'd caught on and knew when to stop, when to crouch, when to crawl, and when to haul ass like I was running from a fire.

We came to another cross street that used to lead to a few fast food restaurants. Bodies on the ground. So many bodies. We crouched at the corner of a building and a street missing a signpost. The whole thing had been run over and was tangled in a heap of twisted metal that used to be car. Now that car was a burned out husk filled with bodies. Must have been a family of six. They were all dead, but still smoking. I gagged at the smell.

Joel grabbed the front of my jump suit and dragged me away.

We rounded a corner and ran smack into a band of them. They turned white eyes on us and commenced with snarling and moaning like a bunch of wild animals. Reynolds shot the nearest one in the chest and then his rifle jammed. Joel tapped him on the shoulder, so he fell back while Joel provided covering fire.

Reynolds worked his gun and then came up shooting. He moved backwards as Kelly also fell back, and then we were on the run again.

We dove into what used to be a fast food restaurant. The place was deserted and trash had been hauled out and scattered all over the floor. A bag of sesame seed buns was split open but covered in blood. I was so hungry I considered rooting around until I found one that hadn't been splattered.

"Think they have food here?"

"Fuck if I know. Sweep the kitchen." Joel nodded at Reynolds.

Joel went low but peeked out a window. The others had been broken out so he avoided those. I stayed next to him while Reynolds moved into the other room. He came back a few seconds later and shook his head.

Joel moved toward him but Reynolds shook his head once again.

"Shit," Joel said and followed Reynolds.

"What?" I asked.

"You don't want to know."

"You really don't," Reynolds said and moved ahead.

"I want to go on record as saying I hate this."

"Yeah, yeah. Quit whining and man up so we can get away from this hellhole."

"Think the cities any better?" I asked.

"Can it be worse?"

He had a point.

We moved out of the building and slid past a small store next door. The entire front had been shot to hell. There was a pile of bodies out front and most didn't twitch. Joel scouted and then held out his hand before crossing in front of it.

"Friendlies!" he said in a low voice. He looked back at us once and then dashed across the field of fire of whoever might be manning a gun inside.

No one shot at him, so we stayed low and followed.

We sprinted to the end of the street and then paused next to a burned out bus. It was white, but flames had turned the outside into shades of black. Soot stuck to my back when I slammed against it. Something fell out of a smashed window and grabbed my neck.

I dropped and let out a little scream of horror. Joel looked from me to the hand and smirked. I followed his eyes and got a look at my assailant. It was a hand, all right, but it was covered in blackened flesh.

"Fuck this," I muttered.

Then the hand twitched.

I could have just leapt right out of my skin but managed to hang onto my sanity by a thread. Fingers moved, grasping at nothing, then they went still again.

We pressed on and found ourselves near an administrative building. Shapes moved behind dark windows.

The place looked familiar and I thought it might have been some kind of processing center for those shipping out to new commands.

"Be ready," Reynolds said.

"Who's in there?"

"Not sure," he said. "But they probably aren't friendly."

We crouched behind a car and went over our weapons. Joel popped his magazine and checked it while Reynolds did the same. Joel laid out an extra mag and then came up in a crouch.

"If they rush us, shoot the first few, then we move. They aren't the fastest things, so we should be able to make it across the street."

"You guys move. I'll cover," Reynolds said.

Luckily, we didn't have to turn the street into a bloodbath.

A pair of guys in green moved out of the building. They had guns like Joel and looked like they knew how to use them. Reynolds looked over the side of the car and then grinned. He whistled once and then put a hand in the air.

The guys snapped to and aimed guns at us. From my vantage point, looking through the remains of a blown out window, I feared they were going to start shooting and ask questions later.

Reynolds held his gun in the air and then rose slowly. Joel did the same.

"Good to see someone's alive," one of the guys said.

We moved on the soldiers' position. Other guys in green filed out of the building. Joel Kelly and Reynolds nodded at them and they nodded back. They went into this weird dance where they looked each other's gear up and down, then exchanged this and that. I saw at least two magazines swapped out for other magazines. Rounds were checked and counted out. Someone handed Kelly a pack that looked like food. He tossed it to me then took one for himself.

"You guys with the eight?" one of the other soldiers asked.

"We just got here," Reynolds said.

We'd moved back into the building the guys had just vacated and crouched in the remains of an overturned trashcan. There were quite a few blood splatters but no bodies, for a change. Not even any parts of bodies.

"What?" One of the guys looked them over. He had steel grey eyes and looked like what an action hero should look like.

"We just got here, Gunny. We were on the McClusky before it rammed into the base."

"I saw that. Damn shame."

"What's going on here?" Joel asked.

"It'd take days to tell you. Something's been hitting cities and bases. The first we heard about it was up north around the Portland area. I guess some Black Water types brought back something besides crotch rot from the desert. At least, that's the rumor."

Joel stared at the man like he was looking at a ghost.

"What was it?" Reynolds asked.

"Don't know. Rumors about some new weapon we were experimenting with."

"Bullshit," Joel stated. "I was over there and those guys don't have the tech."

"True, and don't that make you wonder who does have the tech?"

"But what are we even talking about? This shit. All this fucking shit. It's like a horror movie." Joel gestured around.

"Yeah, it's some shit. We're getting off the base. Chain of command is stuck in limbo. Stay, fight, run, fight. We're tired of taking orders from fifteen people so we're getting gone. You guys want in?" Gunny looked us over. "Who's he?"

They meant me. Did I really stick out that much?

"I'm Petty Officer First Class Creed. Jackson Creed."

Reynolds and Kelly followed my lead and gave introductions.

"A squid? Shit."

"Yeah. I know what you mean. I'd trade all my valuable knowledge of making a ship go fast for some combat training right about fucking now," I said, and there was a lot of truth behind those words.

"Well, you're big and you carry a big stick. Sometimes that's all it takes." Gunny nodded at the wrench in my hand. "How many rounds you got?"

"I don't know. A pocketful and one extra clip."

"Lesson number one, squid. It's called a magazine. A clip is what a girl puts in her hair. You a girl?"

Jesus Christ. I'd been recruited into the Marines and this was boot.

"Right. Magazine. Sure, Gunny."

"I'm just giving you shit." He shot me a half grin. "Cooper. Hook this guy up with some ammunition."

Cooper was older and even bigger than me. He wore enough gear to slow down a camel. Cooper reached into a one of the many pouches that adorned his vest and pulled out a magazine. He looked at my gun and then shrugged and handed it over.

I popped the mag and found the one he'd handed over was a match.

"Here's the drill, gents." Gunny looked between the three of us. "We are getting the fuck out of dodge. Coronado Base is now a death trap, so we're going to leave it behind and take our chances closer to the city. If that doesn't work, then we'll make up the next part, but I will come up with a plan. Got it?"

The guys all Hoo'd and wouldn't you know it? They didn't do a full hoo-ah.

"The plan sounds like shit." Gunny's eyebrows went up at my words. "But it's a hell of a lot better than what we've been doing, which is kind of a circle jerk."

"Right. You're welcome to come up with your own brilliant tactical plan," Gunny said.

The others chuckled. Me and my mouth. If we got off the base, these guys would probably play "string up the squid" and leave me for the dead. That's if they didn't feed me to a horde first.

"I got nothing," I said.

"Great. So, if the General is leaving us in his hands, I suggest we move. Cooper and Walowitz, check the street. Lets get this show on the road."

The two men moved out and advanced up the street. They ran to an overturned car and crouched beside it. One motioned and another team of two went. They ran to an overturned pickup truck and dropped beside it. Two others from Gunny's group took off toward them. When all four were in place, the first two dashed toward a street corner and stuck to the side of the building while the second pair kept watch.

Movement ahead. I snapped the handgun up at the same time as the soldiers by the overturned car. Sounds to the west. Reynolds slipped out and took up position on the corner of the building, then peeked. He slipped his head back, took a couple of deep breaths and peeked again.

Reynolds ran to our position.

"Fuck load of them coming our way."

"Now ain't that a bitch. 'Bout how many?" Gunny squinted into the distance.

"Can't say. Hundred. Maybe more."

Gunny motioned and the others followed. All told, the men plus us made eight. Eight souls that wanted to get the hell out of this area. Seven men better trained than I'd ever been. My on-the-job training had consisted of pointing a gun and shooting. It was easy, the easiest thing in the world. You just had to ignore the fact that there were people on the other end of the barrel.

Cooper split off and went with Reynolds. They rounded the corner of the building and layed down fire. Gunny motioned and we moved toward the fallen car. The two that had been there moved to the end of the street and took up position.

Our routine became one of sending out scouts, shooting whatever dead came our way, and then trying to find an alternate path.

Hundreds had been drawn to the gunfire, but we were also within sight of the base perimeter. The city proper lay out there and it was freakishly quiet.

Eerie.

Dead.

No one trotted over sidewalks. No cars zipped along streets. The navy base was a hub of activity on a slow day. If a ship were returning from a tour, the base would be packed. Now, it was a different story. No one waited at the gate. No one was checking ID's and no one, besides us, seemed to be alive.

"I hate this," I muttered.

"You and me both, brother." Gunny clapped me on the back.

Then they hit us.

It was like everyone I'd just pictured in my mind on a normal day had decided to say hi. They shambled. They crawled. They dragged broken limbs. They pulled themselves along the ground with guts and appendages hanging by scraps of skin. There were so many I couldn't see an end to the mass.

"Not good!" Joel Kelly said.

This guy was a frigging genius.

The Marines opened up on the first row and dropped a number of them. Some got tangled up on their fallen brethren and went down. We angled to the west and then made a run for it. It would actually be more appropriate to say the Marines ran and I tried to keep up. I huffed and puffed and regretted every cigarette I'd ever smoked in my life. I regretted the Thai whiskey I'd inhaled a few days ago.

There was now a mass behind us and another horde to the east. As soon as we hit one more, we'd be truly fucked.

"Movement front!" one of the guys yelled.

We were fucked.

My gut burned and I tasted acid in the back of my throat. If we didn't rest soon, I was gonna puke. If we rested, we were dead.

Gunny yanked his gun and shot a Z between the eyes, then blew another one's head open. I wanted his gun. It had some serious stopping power. They were only ten or fifteen feet away, but he just stood there with his legs spread and dropped two of them. I took a shot as well, but it wasn't as neat. I just wanted to be cool. I wasn't. I was also shaking from being so winded.

The guy I hit flinched to the side, so Gunny shot that asshole, too.

"Move!" he yelled, and his men did just that.

We ran from both herds. A couple of burned out buildings ahead could provide protection but we moved past them.

"What about those?" I huffed.

"Get trapped?" Joel looked over his shoulder to drop the news on me.

That made sense.

We sprinted for a section of fence that still stretched a few hundred feet in both directions. It had a layer of razor wire running along the top and I didn't think any one of us were going to risk getting hung up there, feet dangling while the Z's pulled them back down.

"Get that clear, but just enough to let a man through. We don't want them coming through," Gunny shouted.

Cooper and Walowitz had been on point. They hit the fence and swung packs off their shoulders. Cooper came up with a pair of pliers while Walowitz covered him. A couple of Z's got close so he blasted them. Cooper was one cool fucker. He worked at the fence with quick snips and never lost his concentration.

The pack closed in on us from every direction.

I shot until the gun ran empty, slipped a magazine out and jammed a new one in. Then it was back to blasting. I tried to conserve ammo and take well-aimed shots, but there were just so many and they were so damn close, it was hard not to panic. When panic did set in I did my best to focus on my breathing.

"Good one," Gunny called. He kept the pep talk coming and it helped me focus.

They pushed us toward the fence.

The Marines formed a semi-circle as they fell back.

"We're in business!" Cooper called and slipped through the slit in the chain link fence.

The others crowded around. Panic might have hit one of the guys because he broke rank and dove through.

"Calmly, gentlemen. Christ, Michaels."

I got a push and slithered through the new doorway. Reynolds was next and then Joel Kelly followed him. The others covered us until the Z's were right on them. Gunny shot one in the face, kicked another one in the leg so hard it snapped, then pushed back a pair and shot one in through the throat. Blood exploded and splattered Gunny but he didn't even blink. Two of the men weren't so smooth and got pulled, screaming, into the mess of hands and snarling teeth.

Gunny stood his ground and fought them until his men were through. Then they poked gun barrels through the fence and shot until he could dive under the fence.

He turned, took very careful aim and shot the two men that had been under his command. They both slumped.

"Fuck!" One of the men yelled and shot until his gun ran dry. He dropped the magazine and slapped another one home so fast it made my head spin. He advanced on the fence and fired until Gunny laid a hand on him.

"Move it, people!" he ordered, and we followed toward a road filled with abandoned vehicles.

The outskirts of the base showed signs of battles. There were more bodies but most looked like civilians. We moved among them looking for supplies.

Reynolds moved to point and scouted. Joel stuck by me.

A pair of jets shot overhead. They moved toward the city at high speed and a few seconds later explosions rocked the morning air. We looked up as one and Kelly whistled.

"How bad is it?" Walowitz asked the same question that was on my mind.

"Only one way to find out, and that's to get in the fight."

Men nodded.

"Gunny. My wife's family was staying at a hotel near here. About a mile that way," he said and pointed to the northeast. "I'm going to check on them."

"Stay put, Marine."

"I'm not in your command. Appreciate the assist, gentlemen, but I have to know."

No one said a word as he walked away at a fast clip.

"Gunny?" Cooper asked.

"What am I supposed to do, shoot him in the back?" He looked between the men but they didn't say a word.

Reynolds whistled from ahead and motioned. Gunny moved out and the others followed, but they strung out and kept their eyes everywhere at once.

It was less than five minutes before we ran into a real shit storm.

We slid between buildings and empty cars. Streets covered in debris. Bodies that moved and others that lay still. We moved quickly and used shops or hotels as cover when we had to.

Gunny took us to a four lane cross street that still had a couple of moving cars; they ignored us and navigated between wrecks and abandoned vehicles.

"Let's commandeer us a few cars," Gunny said.

That was the best idea I'd heard all day.

"Shit, Gunny. How are we gonna navigate around all these wrecks?"

"I guess we get out and push when we have to," Walowitz said.

"Are we Marines or Triple A? We'll find a vehicle of sufficient size and drive over anyone that gets in our way," Cooper said.

Gunny chuckled and nodded.

The group spread out. Joel stuck by my side while I checked out a couple of trucks. There was a huge eighteen-wheeler partially on the road and partly on the shoulder. I approached and jumped up on the ladder to see if anyone was inside. A man in a faded green t-shirt threw himself at me. He clawed at the door while I tried to stuff my stomach back down my throat.

We moved away.

Cooper and Reynolds poked inside a pair of cars but shook their heads. Cooper checked three more before finding one to his liking. It was a huge SUV that could probably seat eight comfortably. He pulled a corpse out—an elderly woman with blue hair. She was clothed in a huge dress that was more of a nightgown. When he released the body she hit the ground, but her hand grabbed his arm and she pulled herself up. Teeth clamped onto skin.

Cooper turned, eyes filled with horror. He looked at the wound and then did something I thought I could never do. He dropped his assault rifle, ripped the handgun out of his holster, put it under his chin, and pulled the trigger.

I looked away, and it was a good thing I did. From the base, the mass that had tried to attack us had somehow made it through the fence. They moved toward us, arms extended in claws, mouths snarling, teeth covered in blood.

"Move!" Gunny yelled.

We angled off the road and raced toward the city.

That's when the second mass came upon us.

It was like we were stuck between two groups of angry football fans and we were the opposing team.

We ran.

The second horde was already on us. They got one of the guys whose name I didn't know. He went down with a scream and a few seconds later something exploded.

Bodies flew, but it wasn't enough to stem the tide.

Gunny palmed a grenade and tossed one to Walowitz. They both pulled pins and threw at the same time.

The effect was devastating to the front lines that didn't even know to lift their hands or drop to the ground to protect appendages. Joel and I took shelter behind a car but popped back up. I followed his lead and didn't deviate from doing the exact same shit he was doing. If he dropped his pants and popped a squat right there, I would have been beside him doling out the toilet paper.

Gunny led the charge with Walowitz and the other two Marines behind them. They fired, moved in, fired, and when they were close enough they drew side arms and shot until the entire front line had disintegrated.

Reynolds broke away first and dashed to our side. The others followed, but they fired as they went.

Joel took aim and blasted anyone that fell under his sights. The dead dropped like flies, but still the mass advanced. At least with the first rank down, we had created enough of a mess to hang them up.

That's when I saw the first one.

The guy crept along the ground on all fours. He didn't really speak, he just gibbered like he was talking to himself in a shrieking laugh. It was unnerving. The worst was when he leapt off the ground and hit one of the Marines. They both went down in a heap; the Marine got the best of the engagement, but not before having part of his throat ripped out.

"Retreat!" Gunny yelled and we hauled ass.

We hit a roadblock a hundred and fifty feet later. We came up along a side street, hung a hard left to avoid a fresh horde, and hit a location that held five or six military vehicles. No one manned them, but they made a hell of a choke point because they stretched between two buildings and blocked the entire street.

Joel leapt on top of a HUMVEE and fired while we stayed behind cover. He took out a few but they were gaining on our tired asses. I was so tired I seriously considered just becoming one of them so I wouldn't have to be scared and exhausted any more.

I scrambled up the side of a transport and swung myself onto the roof. I'd fired my last round and hefted my wrench. The first shuffler that came after me got a face full of steel.

Walowitz and Gunny dove into a transport and shut the door. The vehicle was soon surrounded. Joel and I backed up as Gunny saluted us. A few seconds later the engine roared to life and they backed up. Gunny rolled down the window an inch and shouted at us. "Try for the park in two days at eleven PM."

His truck came to a halt as more and more of them piled on. He shrugged, saluted again, and roared into the crowd. Gunny rolled down his window a few more inches, stuck out his arm, and pounded the side of the cab. "Come on you fuckers!" he yelled.

We didn't wait around to see how far he got.

Reynolds and another Marine joined us as we crawled on top of trucks and then slid down the other sides. The Marine – whose name may have been Jonas – slipped and fell off the side of a truck. He cried out, but before we could get him he was covered in Z's.

They were on all sides now as we stood in the flatbed of a truck that had been used as some kind of transport. Joel tossed his gun and picked up another. I found a handgun but didn't pay attention to the make. I just yanked it out of an unused holster, ignoring the corpse it was attached to, and shot the first dead fuck that fell under my sights.

Reynolds kicked one in the face but she latched onto his leg and her mouth darted in to bite him. I thought the fabric of his camo gear may have protected him, but he kicked her again and backed up in horror.

"We are so screwed!" Joel said.

The rest had reached the truck. A hundred clawing hands on every side.

I don't know if it was the stress of the dying Marines, the loss of Gunny, or just the culmination of the entire day. More than likely, it was the bite. Reynolds got this wild look in his eye and told us to get ready.

I thought he meant that we should get ready to die. Reynolds grabbed a bandolier covered in green balls and slung it around his waist. He took a couple off and handed them to Joel.

Joel Kelly took them and flipped Reynolds a questioning look, then shot a Z in the face.

Reynolds ran to the end of the flat bed and leapt like he was going to crowd-surf. His fingers worked at his belt as he went, and when he came off the truck he left behind a tinkling pile of clips.

"DOWN!" Joel yelled and pushed me to the floor.

It was the most incredible act of heroism I have ever seen. Reynolds threw himself into the maelstrom and saved us.

The blast was immense. What was left wasn't fit to bury. It would need to be scooped up and burned.

We used the explosion as cover and ran through the fresh passageway. When a pair of the dead came around a corner, Joel blasted one in half and then threw the empty assault rifle at the other. I didn't look, but I knew Joel was close to losing it.

Joel and I ran until I was gasping for air and shaking like a leaf. We'd left the mass behind but we were in a new part of the city, somewhere I'd never seen before.

An hour later we found the partially boarded up two-story house and founded Fortress.

05:45 hours approximate
Location: San Diego CA – Roz's Roof

That's enough for today. It's early morning and I'd love to get some more shuteye, but the sun is rising. One of the shufflers keeps throwing himself at the side of the garage. I wish Joel would get up and shoot the fucker between the eyes.

Craig and Christy look miserable. They've already eaten the few snacks they managed to get out of the house. I didn't say anything, but I had nothing stashed in my bag except this log, a few magazines, and my wrench.

Noise to the north. I think it's a chopper. If it comes anywhere near us, I'm giving up the hiding technique and jumping up and down like a maniac.

This is Machinist Mate First Class Jackson Creed and I am still alive.

FREE RIDE

11:25 hours approximate
Location: San Diego, CA – Roz's Roof

Supplies:

- Food: zip
- Weapons: almost zip
- Attitude: messy

I tried to sleep. Tried.

It was a losing battle. The moment I closed my eyes all I heard were the dead. They milled, staggered, walked into the garage wall, and every five to ten minutes a shuffler launched itself at the roof.

The truth was that I was too damn scared to sleep. If I were really tired enough I'd have dozed off hours ago. Instead, adrenalin kicked my nerves up a notch. A side effect was that I felt like shit. My muscles ached from being clenched and my mind was filled with all the horrible things I'd seen over the course of two weeks. From a narrow escape aboard the USS McClusky to fighting for our lives in the very garage we were stranded on, and all of the terrible shit in between.

Roz huddled up next to Joel Kelly. I didn't take it as a slight, even though I'd saved her life. Joel had saved my life quite a few times and I'd saved his. I think. Yeah, I probably pulled his ass out of a few bad situations. Kinda hard to survive in this ridiculous world if you aren't helping keep your best buddy from becoming zombie chow.

She didn't exactly invite him she just happened to lay down next to him. Joel was snoring away and rolled onto his side. She was close and they ended up with their arms over each other. How she could sleep through his snoring was beyond me. How any of us could sleep.

I didn't get jealous. Why should I? It's not like she and I were together. We had that little hug and ass grab yesterday in the garage, but we both thought we were about to die. Even if we had made it back inside, I doubted I had the balls to go after her. They were too busy being shrunk up inside my gut in fear.

I rolled over again and tried to fix the lumps that made up my backpack. Then I tried to doze on my arm but it fell asleep. I rolled onto my stomach and got a face full of leaves and dirt. If I wasn't mistaken, there was even a layer of moss up here that I was now inhaling.

"Can you eat moss?" I asked, voice low.

"Gross, dude," Craig said.

"I'm starving, man and pretty soon a bowl of moss stew might look good to you too," I said. "Maybe a bowl of moss stew with pork belly to add some salt."

"Pork belly? Sounds just as gross," he whispered back.

"It's just another name for bacon."

"I'd kill a guy for some bacon."

My stomach rumbled in response.

Hours passed and I may have dozed. My ankle ached like a bitch and the rest of my body wasn't much better. The next time I run into a fucking zombie apocalypse, I plan to bring some serious painkillers to the party. Not to mention a duffle bag filled with Twinkies and MREs. Yeah, I'd eat the hell out of some MREs right now.

We had quite a few of them. The problem? They were in a house filled with the dead, so that idea was just as fucking dead. Going back into the house wasn't happening unless we figured out a way to go in Ironman-style, complete with metal suit and weaponry. The way these undead assholes acted, they'd probably drag us down, iron suit or not.

I don't remember when, but I finally fell asleep and got an hour or two of REM. Good for fucking me.

06:00 hours approximate
Location: San Diego CA – Roz's Roof

I woke up with a pounding headache. My ankle was swollen from last night's activities. My back hurt from sleeping on the roof. My shoulder barely worked thanks to falling asleep on my own arm.

I rubbed my eyes but it didn't help. They still felt like sand paper.

"You might have gotten uglier," Joel observed.

I didn't have the energy to flip him off.

"I feel like shit."

"Dehydrated. You need water. We all do," he said.

Joel crept to the edge of the roof and looked over the side of the building. He came back up and shook his head. Roz stayed low and stared after him. The kids were a few feet away, conferring in whispered voices.

It was overcast, and from the chill in the air I'd guess it was no later than about 0600 hours.

"Not good. We can't get down. We can't go back in the garage, and we can't get in the house."

"Still full of dead fucks?"

"Yep," he said. "Craig reconnoitered earlier."

"Brave kid."

"And he's light. Don't want a fresh hole in the roof."

Another helicopter thundered against the morning sky. I'd put it at a mile or two out. We could see it, but it couldn't see us, because we were a speck in a big old pile of fuck you. Too bad we couldn't set a home on fire to signal the chopper.

"Anyone got a flare gun?" I asked.

Joel Kelly rolled his eyes.

The chopper cut to the east and then zipped into the distance until we couldn't hear it anymore.

The morning brought some fog and a creepy view of the world below. Where we'd seen the undead on the ground, now they seemed to be creeping out of the mist with heads and arms floating. A shuffler appeared out of the fog with a leap and then was gone, five or six feet away like some kind of fucked up zombie frog.

The nearest house was twenty or thirty feet away and no matter how fast we could run, there was no way in hell we'd make that sprint. The dead were too thick. I'd have a better chance of pogo-sticking off heads than outrunning the tightly packed horde.

"What if one of us put on a lot of clothes? Then the bites wouldn't get through," Christy said.

"You'd be dragged down and torn apart," I said.

Not a good way to go. Sure they might not be able to bite, yet, but enough of those things on top of the kid and they'd have his arms and legs separated from his torso in no time.

"Uh. Yeah. Bad idea," Christy said.

"Can we make a rope out of our clothes and hook it to the house over there?" Craig pointed at the nearest rooftop.

Poor kid. He looked worse than me. His hair was a mess but his eyes were the really sad part. He must have been rubbing at them because one was dark red and he looked as tired as anyone I'd ever seen. Craig lifted one hand to point at the house but it hung limp, almost like a Z's hand. Even his words were slurred.

"One, I don't want to be dangling buck ass naked over those bastards. A shuffler would surely get us. Two, none of us can possibly James Bond the rope over there."

"It was just a suggestion," he said and frowned. Craig lay back down and stared in the direction of the slow rising sun.

"Yeah. It was a good one," I said, but he didn't acknowledge my words.

Joel looked at me but I could only shrug.

The sound of a helicopter again. I sat up and tried to get a glimpse but couldn't tell which direction it was coming from.

"There!" Joel said. He was up on his knees pointing west of San Diego, out toward the water.

The chopper cut across my vision like a fucking messiah. If Jesus himself had risen from the ground and taken to the air, I don't think I'd have been this excited.

The thundering grew louder. The big green military transport did a zig-zag over buildings and roads. As it moved I found myself getting up. First, one foot under a knee. Then I was up in a crouch and trying to ignore the pain in my ankle. I licked my dry lips, but it didn't help, even though I was, for some reason, salivating.

"Is it coming this way?" Roz moved beside me and put her hand on my waist.

I looked her way and tried not to grin like a crazy man.

"Yeah. It's coming our way."

It was. I thought for sure it would go anywhere else but it kept doing a serpentine strut across the sky. Its general direction was still toward us.

I jumped to my feet and waved my hands in the air and started to shout.

"Hey! Hey! We're right fucking here!"

Roz did the same and so did the kids. Craig didn't get to his feet but he waved. His hand was nearly as listless as his body. I hoped the poor kid wasn't sick.

Thank the fuck Christ someone was coming. I was worried about the kid. I'd just met him a day or two ago but he and his sister didn't deserve this crazy new world. I couldn't help but wonder if this part of the country was infected but the rest of the world was fine and dandy. Maybe families were rising even now to have breakfast together. To watch the morning news or sit through children's cartoons. Mom and Dad rushing off to work while the kids try to stay awake in school.

I shook my head and made my brain focus on the task at hand—getting that chopper's attention.

The helicopter must have seen us because they made a beeline straight toward Roz's house.

There was one side effect of our antics and shouts of joy. The horde below had gone into a frenzy. They pressed in on the sides of the garage and howled for our blood. A pair of shufflers flung themselves at the building like we were a side of bacon left out for their morning meal.

The chopper slowed as it neared us. It was green and had large side doors. One was open and had a machine gun pointed out just like they were in a war zone – and that wasn't far from the truth.

The pilot and co-pilot were hard to make out, but I was sure one of them nodded in our direction. A face appeared behind them and studied us intently.

The wash of the blades as the helicopter came to hover in front of us blew Joel Kelly's FDNY cap off his head. He waved but the pilots didn't wave back.

The chopper swung to the side and my gut twisted.

"No!" I screamed. "Don't leave us!"

Roz jumped up and down but I couldn't hear her over the rush of wind.

The side door came into view and with it, the big machine gun. I thought for a crazy moment that they were about to open up on us.

The man that I'd seen a few seconds ago leaned out and waved. He was tall and had dark hair laced with grey. He looked like Gunny, but this man was older. He waved again and we waved back. I felt dumb for it, but it was the best I had in place of a hug and a wet kiss. I'd save that for after we were rescued.

The helicopter hovered just out of reach, then the guy hanging onto the doorway motioned for us to get down. I didn't need a second invitation and dropped to a crouch on my sore ankle. It screamed in pain but I pushed it to the back of my mind.

The man produced a bullhorn and fiddled with the buttons. A woman dressed in combat gear moved beside him and said something. He nodded at her and then lifted a bullhorn.

"Stay down just like that. When we get close make your way onto the craft. When you are onboard sit down and don't move. Got it?"

I gave the thumbs up. He nodded at us and then yelled something at the pilots.

Roz knelt while she talked to the kids. Christy looked at Craig and gave his hand a quick squeeze.

The dead around us went into a frenzy. The shuffler that had haunted us all night tried to leap onto the helicopter but it was a good twelve feet off the ground. The down draft from the blades flattened a couple that were on shaky limbs, or worse, were missing them entirely.

The horde moved in on us again and pressed against the side of the garage. They beat at it and moaned. Even with the immense noise it was truly a fucking chorus of the damned.

Joel prodded Craig and pointed at the edge of the roof. Craig took Christy's hand and together they crept toward the side of the building. He kept his hand in front of his face while she stayed low and let Craig take most of the wash. When they were close enough to step on to the strut, a guy inside reached out, grabbed her arm, and hauled Christy inside.

Craig collapsed when Christy was gone. He didn't move, just sat there with his legs folded under his butt.

The dead went into a fresh frenzy when they saw their prize getting away. The shuffler howled and gibbered. He leapt at the building over and over until he was bloody. The other's pressed from all sides.

Roz was next with Joel helping her toward the end. They tried to prod Craig but he pushed hands away.

The building shook and a corner of the roof swayed, then collapsed as the wall beneath it gave way. Roz made it to the helicopter strut and was helped on board.

The roof tilted but didn't go down. I grabbed Craig and hauled him to his feet.

"Come on. We're almost there!" I yelled.

He nodded once and said something but I couldn't make out the words.

Hands helped him onboard as the roof tilted again. I leaned forward and barely kept my feet. One quick glance over my shoulder told me that this was going to be a very short day if I didn't get my sorry ass on the chopper.

I grabbed my backpack and swung it over my back. The huge wrench got me right in the kidney. I almost doubled over in pain. Then I moved to the edge of the roof and prepared to avoid being zombie chow.

There was a moment where Joel and I met eyes. He prodded me onboard, but I did the same. We stared back at each other like a pair of idiot heroes in a buddy action movie. I didn't feel particularly heroic. All I really wanted to do was get on the helicopter, get to somewhere safe, and take a long shit because my sphincter was not up to the business of me being scared to death all the goddamn time.

Joel pushed and I advanced on the chopper. It was only a few feet away but below was a mass of dead like I'd never seen before. All eyes were on me as I stepped toward the helicopter strut.

The older man's hand came out and I got one foot on the strut while my other was still on the roof. That's when the damn thing gave in. Joel managed to make it to the edge but the second wall crumbed to kindling beneath us.

The shifting caused me to end up stretched between two worlds with hell directly underneath. Someone grabbed the guy in the transport, and with that as an anchor, he hauled me, screaming, into the helicopter.

Joel held on for dear life, and behind him came the dead. The collapsed roof had created a perfect platform to serve him up like dinner. The Z's moved up the newly created ramp while Joel looked on in horror.

"We can't risk it. That building's gonna collapse any minute and probably take us with it!" The woman in the chopper yelled over the "whump whump" of the blades.

The older man looked at us. I had taken a seat on the floor but when I saw Joel's panicked face I came to my feet.

"You can't leave him. He's saved all of us more than once."

"Sorry, son," he said and leaned over to say something to the pilot.

I didn't think. I pushed him to the side and stepped back onto the helicopter strut. I used the machine gun barrel as an anchor and stretched out for Joel.

"Get off! I can't shoot if you're in the way!" the woman said.

"Good!" I bellowed back.

I reached over my shoulder and ripped the huge wrench out and swung it around to lean out as far as I could.

Joel got one hand on the wrench head. Another garage wall went down and took the roof with it.

Z's scrambled for purchase but slid down the platform with arms and legs flailing.

Except for one.

The shuffler was nasty. He had long strands of hair but they weren't enough to cover his head. They hung over his face like wisps of white cotton. I shuddered because he made a leap, mouth open, and managed to reach the edge of the garage wall that Joel was balanced on.

I pulled as hard as I could and Joel came along for the ride. The man grabbed my arm and pulled me in. I pulled Joel along until he was on the helicopter strut. The engine screamed above us as all of our weight settled and pulled the transport closer to the collapsing building.

Joel got his hand on the side of the chopper and pulled himself inside. I struggled against the tilting chopper and managed to get one leg in before the shuffler leapt.

We were rising when it caught the strut and managed to hold on. The helicopter tilted once again and suddenly I was looking down at about a hundred hungry mouths.

"Asshole!" I yelled and kicked the shuffler in the face. I did it again and he fell away into the crowd.

They hauled me in and all I could do was collapse as my heart thundered within my chest in rhythm to the blades above us.

After a few deep breaths I looked up into the face of a grinning Marine named Joel Kelly.

"I am not cut out for this fucking hero bullshit!" I yelled.

"Me either, man. But I love you just the same."
He clapped my shoulder one time then took a seat.

The old man looked us over appraisingly but
didn't say a word.

"Thanks for saving us," I said after I'd
managed to catch my breath. "I'm Jackson Creed
and my gay lover there is Marine Sergeant Joel
Kelly."

The man nodded at us.

"I'm not his gay...whatever, man. Thanks for
picking us up."

"You folks were about to be zombie chow."

"Yeah. Not much choice. We were stuck up
there until you came along."

"I'd like to get real friendly but we gotta make
sure you're safe. This won't take long so save the
introductions. I'd hate to shake hands and then have
to blow your brains out." He grinned, but there was
no humor behind the gesture.

The guy nodded at the gunner. She slid a silver
metal box about the size of a briefcase out from
under the metal bench. The guy took it from her and
opened it to reveal a computer display. There was a
camera attached by a bunch of wires. Shit looked
like a science lab experiment.

"We just need a picture of your eye," he said
and extended the camera.

"A picture?"

"Yep. We figured out how to spot the virus.
Doesn't always set in right away. I've seen guys
walk around infected for three days before turning."

"Damn," I said and submitted to a shot.

The flash was bright and left me blinking furiously for a few seconds.

We took turns opening an eye wide while he snapped a shot. After each picture he typed something on a keyboard and waited.

"Where're we headed?" I asked.

"We have a base but it's not much. Damn zeek's nearly overrun it every day. All the ammo in the world and we can't keep clear of them. Piles and piles of the dead. Never smelled anything so foul in my life."

The sound of the rotor overhead was a constant throb against the cabin as I peered over the lid of the silver box to see if I could get a peek at the display.

"What's going on out there?" I asked.

"Out there? Out in the world you mean? How long you boys been stuck out here?"

Roz cleared her throat.

"Sorry miss." He smiled in her direction.

"No problem." She grinned back but it was just as empty of humor.

"Almost two weeks. Our ship crashed into the base. We've been on the run ever since." Joel filled in the details.

"I'll tell you what's going on out there." He looked at each of us in the eye. "The worst things you can imagine. When you think it can't get worse, it does. When you think that humanity can't get any worse, it does. And when you think the damned Z's can't get any nastier."

The man stared hard at the screen and then swallowed.

"They do."

"Are we good?" Jackson nodded toward the screen.

Craig and Christy looked on with wide eyes. They were huddled together on the hard metal bench.

"Oh, we're good." The guy smiled.

He moved toward the door opposite the machine gun and looked outside.

"Don't be scared, kids." He smiled at Christy and Craig. "Come here, bud. I'll show you something that will make you feel better."

Craig had been slumped against the wall. He stared into space like she hadn't heard the man.

"Here you go." The older man smiled and produced one of those juice boxes with the little plastic straw glued to the side. It was all I could do not to leap across the tiny space and tear it out of his hand.

Craig made a little noise and slipped off the bench.

I slid my backpack off and pushed it into a corner and got a glance at our rescuer's boots. Instead of military issue he was wearing something out of a cowboy movie. Were those snakeskin boots? Talk about an action hero come to life.

Joel had lost his assault rifle in the excitement and looked like his best friend had died. Glad that wasn't true, since I was probably the closest thing to a best friend he'd ever had.

"So who are you?" I asked over the loud thumping of the rotor blades.

The smell of gas and oil filled the cabin but it was whisked away in a blast as air as the man that had rescued us slid the door open.

"Hey man, that's loud."

The guy didn't say a word. He grabbed Craig by the back of the neck, and pulled him all the way off the bench. He looked at the guy in silent shock, but his silence turned into a scream as the man threw Craig out of the doorway.

"The fuck!" Joel Kelly came off the seat just as I tried to stand. He reached for a non-existent side arm. I went for my bag because I was going to haul out eight pounds of metal and bush his fucking head in!

The machine gunner pulled her gun but Joel did some Marine shit. He swiped her arm up and locked his hand over hers. She didn't sit around for that and fought back.

Christy hauled off and threw a poorly aimed punch but the guy slid aside and knocked the girl to the hard floor.

"Knock it off back there!" The pilot turned his head to shout at us.

I ripped my wrench free of the backpack but there was no room to swing it in the tiny cabin.

Roz stared on in shock and then covered her face with her hands and sobbed.

The guy who had just tossed Craig to his death pulled out a huge gun and pointed it at my head. My resolve deflated, as did my grip on the wrench. The fight went out of me. I was done. The days of running and hiding piled on top of the escape, combined with Craig's sudden death nearly made me pass out.

"Stop this!" the guy yelled. "Stop it now or there's gonna be a lot more blood."

"Ouch, bastard!" the gunner said.

"Sails! Enough!" the man with the huge gun pointed at me said.

Joel Kelly managed to get the gun away from the gunner, Sails, and none to gently. He got a look at the big barrel pointed my way and he relaxed his grip on the woman and lowered the gun.

She must not have taken too kindly to Joel's rough handling because she slapped him.

"He's trying to help. You don't know what's going on here, asshole," she said and rubbed her wrist.

"What about what's going on here? He just tossed a teenage boy out the goddamn door. That's what's going on here. I don't know how you people are used to dealing with civilians but you don't just kill them."

"You don't? Is that right, son? How many have you killed since this all began?"

"I killed Z's. The dead. I didn't kill innocent people."

He kept the gun pointed at my head but turned the box to face us and lifted the lid. A laptop screen was set into a hard foam backing. The screen had an image of the inside of an eyeball. I'd seen something like this when I got my eyes checked a few years ago.

"What the fuck are we looking at?" Joel rubbed his face where the gunner had smacked him.

"This is your friend that I just tossed. See the dark spots? Those are dead cells. A lot of dead cells. In a few more days or maybe hours – hell, could be minutes, he would have turned. You want a Z in here? You wanna be stuck with a monster in this tiny little box? No you do not."

"Craig was fine!" Christy went crazy.

She lashed out and caught the guy across the nose with the back of her fist. It wasn't a great shot, but it got the job done. The man fell back and a shot rang out in the cabin. I sucked in a breath expecting a bullet to be lodged in me, but it wasn't. The shot went high and punched through the canopy.

The man pushed Christy against the wall hard, and she collapsed like a sack of potatoes.

Joel wanted to go nuts; I saw it in his eyes and the way his fists clenched on the bench seat. The gunner ripped her gun tight then put it to Joel's head.

"Listen to him. He knows what he's talking about."

Something coughed and the helicopter shuddered. A light flashed in my periphery and then alarms sounded. I didn't need to, but I followed everyone's eyes to the top of the chopper where a hole whistled air. What were the chances?

"Oh shit!" Sails said.

The pilot punched buttons and swore. Our ride swayed one way and then the other. I got slammed against the door and then went flat so it wouldn't happen again. When the chopper tilted to the side I got a look at a huge stadium filled with white tents. Figures moved around the location, but from their wobbling, I assumed none of them were alive. I wasn't sure, but thought it was probably the old Balboa stadium.

Joel held on for dear life as the chopper went into a slow spin.

The pilot did something because we managed to straighten out for all of two seconds before our craft hit the ground. Hard.

I was lifted into the air and smashed into the deck. Breath left my body and I had a hell of a time getting it back.

The gunner had been smashed against the side of the craft and lolled in Joel's lap. The man who'd saved us seemed to be the only one unharmed. He grabbed Christy's form and ripped the door open. The pilot swore, hit some buttons and then ditched.

"This way!" The guy yelled to us as he kept his hold on Christy.

I struggled to my knees while Joel got Sails out of the door. The pilots fell out one after another and then they were on our feet.

I snatched up my backpack and hit the ground right behind them, staggering on my already aching ankle.

No time to rest. No time to worry about the pain shooting up my leg in waves.

"There. It's not far!" The guy picked up Christy and shrugged him over his shoulder. He pointed at a fence

Joel smacked Sails, none too gently. She stirred, looked at him and snarled. Jeez. She looked like one of them for a second. Girl would be cute if she wasn't pointing guns and hitting people.

On the run again? That could mean only one thing.

I looked back and there they were.

There were at least fifty of them. Maybe more. Howling, screaming, and moaning, they walked, crawled, and dragged body parts. They were covered in blood and filth. They were the worst of the worst and they all wanted us.

Not only that, but two shufflers came at us.

I had a vague sense of where we were in relation to the base and San Diego itself, and if I wasn't mistaken, the huge buildings ahead of us were part of the naval medical center. There was a bunch of activity around it as military trucks, transports, and gun-toting HUMVEEs moved around the perimeter of a huge metal fence.

If I were lucky I'd have time to marvel at the construction later. For now I had to actually make it.

We ran our asses off.

If we were in good shape, fresh off the rack, it might have been a cake walk to sprint to the finish line. Not today. I was running on empty. Joel was in bad shape and he had Sails to carry. Roz looked like someone had just punched her in the stomach. The only one that seemed capable of moving was the asshole and he was carrying Christy over his shoulder. I had the urge to sprint and bash in the fuckers head and leave him for the Z's but my ankle barely left me room to stagger at a half sprint.

We might not make it anyway. None of us.

The first of the dead were on us.

Joel slung Sails to the side and fired her gun. He hit a Z right in the chest, dropping him for now. The guy carrying Christy turned and fired a couple of shots dropping a zombie that snarled in our wake.

Roz paused but I motioned her on. There was no point in here trying to be a hero with no weapon.

A shuffler jumped.

I ripped the wrench up in an arc that terminated with the bastards head. He went down, but it was a temporary respite. There were dozens of dead on our heels.

More gun shots and I used what little energy I had left to sprint forward until I reached Roz. I touched her shoulder.

"Just like last night, eh?"

"Fuck this!" she said in reply.

It wouldn't be long now and I didn't even have a gun to finish me and Roz off before they got us. The horde was going to rip us apart.

Gunshots from ahead and several Z's fell. More shots and more bodies dropped.

Holy shit! The cavalry had arrived.

A full contingent of military advanced on our position. Beautiful men and women in full combat gear and packing enough heat to start a war in some third world country.

I did the smart thing and dropped to my knees, dragging Roz down with me.

It was over in seconds. They must have fired five or six hundred rounds but they stopped the horde in its tracks. Even a shuffler, so frightening to us before, was taken down with at least half a dozen bullets.

The trek to the base wasn't as hectic now that help had arrived.

The guy that had rescued us and killed Craig talked to someone that looked like they were in charge. He pointed at us and at the helicopter. A group broke away and headed toward the transport no doubt to see if it was worth trying to fix before being overrun with dead.

The grass here was trampled flat. There was a road running near the base but it was packed with military transports either coming or going. Engines rumbled around us and it felt good to not only be alive but to be back near something resembling civilization with living people moving around.

The guy met us as we stumbled to the bases entrance and he didn't look happy. He'd handed over Christy to one of the men at the gate. He spoke to the man for a few seconds then shrugged the listless body off his shoulder. Another soldier joined them and helped carry Christy into the base.

The man spun on us.

"Listen to me and listen well. This ain't fucking lala land. You know that if you been in the city for any amount of time. There is a shit storm of hate just waiting to suck us all in and we can't take any chances. Got that? No chances. On any other day I'd leave all of you to the dead. That stunt almost cost us all our lives. You do some shit like that again and I'll put a bullet in your head myself."

"You didn't have to do it!" I yelled back. This guy could have been a fucking admiral for all I cared. All I wanted to do was kick his ass.

"This base is secure. No one with a hint of the virus gets in but they get out. In pieces."

"Fucking asshole," I said.

Joel touched my shoulder to pull me back but I wasn't having it. This guy was tall and he looked commanding but I was still a hell of a lot bigger than him. I hefted the wrench but Joel pushed my hand down. I looked at him and he shook his head.

"I am that, but I'm also one alive fucking asshole. Now do yourself a favor and stay alive too. We need every able body we can find. Don't forget. I'm the one who rescued you."

"Oh I won't forget everything you've done. What's your name, anyway?" I gritted my teeth.

He turned to leave, snake skin boots kicking up dirt as he strolled away. He looked over his shoulder and fixed me with his eyes.

"Names Lee and that's all you need to know for now. Good luck, soldier," he said and strolled into a gate that opened for him.

"I'm gonna kill that son-of-a-bitch," I muttered.

"Get in line," Joel said.

Together with Roz, the injured gunner named Sails, and Joel, we limped into the base before the sliding chain link fence rattled closed.

This is Machinist Mate First Class Jackson Creed and I am still alive.

NEW FRIENDS

10:30 hours approximate
Location: San Diego CA – US Naval Hospital

Supplies:

- Food: warm and enough to fill our guts
- Weapons: plenty to go around
- Attitude: I want to punch stuff

All through our lousy time on Roz's garage roof, I thought we were going to die. I thought we were going to slowly starve to death or the Z's would figure out a way to get at us. Instead we were rescued. The dead were doing their best to batter down the house and even succeeded, once the chopper arrived. I don't know if it was all the noise or us being visible. They went into a frenzy and smashed down the damn walls as we flew away.

The entry to the base was so heavily fortified that we had to be escorted in. Every couple of feet there was a pole covered in razor wire and a lot of that wire was covered in flesh, blood splatters, and strips of clothing. It was the perfect trap. If some of the shamblers made it as far as the base, a lot of them would get hung up, then shot by the heavily armed guards patrolling the massive chain-link gate.

The entrance had fortifications and machine guns. Big fuckers with barrels large enough to take down any target on foot. Men and women stood at guard or knelt and stared down barrels. A few shot us dirty looks. Not my fault! I wanted to protest but it seemed prudent to get my smelly ass into the base and blend in, then figure out how to introduce Lee to my eight pounds of wrench.

As we approached the entrance a squad met us. They had an apparatus similar to the one Lee had used. They didn't point guns at us but they looked ready to draw and shoot at the slightest hint of trouble.

After getting the eye treatment we were escorted to a table where a woman took our name and a drop of blood.

"Does the blood tell you if we got it?"

"Maybe," she replied. She looked tired under a mess of black hair.

"That's reassuring," I said.

"I wish we knew more but we don't. We just look for certain anti-bodies. It's easier to see with the magnifying glass. The disease sets up shop and causes clots. Clots show up as red spots. The clots die and the eyes turn white."

"Thanks for the lesson, Doc." Joel said.

"Oh, I'm no doctor." She attempted to smile and then went back to writing notes on a pad of paper.

They tagged us with some numbers and sent us on our way in the general direction of food and water. I limped behind Joel on my screaming ankle.

By the gates were a huge pile of fence sections and a couple of pieces of heavy equipment, including a huge bulldozer and a crane.

Our rescue had been messy, but that's been life since we arrived in Undeadville, USA. At the time I was actually hopeful that when we set foot on the chopper, our would-be rescuer, Lee, would take us to safety. All of us, not just some of us. Then that fucker threw Craig out of the chopper like he was a bag of trash.

The question ate away at me, though. Was Craig one of them? If we'd been stuck on that roof for a few more days would he have changed? It's possible, but he said he was fine, even if he was tired and just plain out of it. Since we'd found the kids they'd been sorta upbeat all things considered.

I didn't see any bite marks on Craig so how the hell had it happened? Was the disease being spread by some new mechanism? For the last ten days we'd seen men and women bitten, look horrified, and within moments become one of the Z's. Now there was a new way for victims to carry the virus?

After the chopper crash, they let us in the front gate. From the looks, as we hauled ass toward safety, I had a feeling they wanted to send us a bill and make us haul the remains of the chopper inside the base.

I was happy that the pilot and co-pilot weren't near us. I was afraid they'd point the finger at us and say it was our fault. The entire battle inside the chopper had taken half a minute. Then we'd struck the ground. I asked Joel Kelly later if he'd ever been in anything like that before.

"A chopper crash? Shit. Been in a few. That one wasn't bad. I'd call it a shaker, but not quite a bone rattler."

I grinned back at his grin and wondered if he was bullshitting me. Only a boneshaker? When we hit it felt like someone had picked me up and thrown me against a brick wall.

Roz moved alongside us while Christy fell into step but she kept glancing over her shoulder as we made our way toward the base.

"Don't think about it," Roz said.

"What if he's okay? We weren't that high; maybe Craig hit something soft." Christy whined from behind us.

"He didn't survive." Roz fell back a step and put a hand around his shoulder. "I'm sorry."

Christy shrugged it off and moved a few feet away.

"Nothing we can do about it now except get that son of a bitch that killed Craig." I tried to sound reassuring.

"He's out there. I know it," she said. "Everyone else in my life is dead. Craig was all I had left."

She had a point, but I couldn't think of anything to say so I let her talk.

"We didn't ask for this. None of this. I shouldn't even be here. I should be home doing school work or playing video games with my friends. I'm so sick of this. So sick of all of this. I hate this world."

"Yeah. Me too. But you gotta go on and honor Craig's memory. If you're gone who's going to remember him?" I asked.

When we were all gone, who would remember us?

"You guys lost?"

I turned to find an unexpected face. With her helmet off she wasn't bad looking, in an "I'll rip your balls off if you cross me" way that I kinda liked. What I didn't like was the fact that she'd helped Lee kill a kid. I also didn't like that she'd hit me hard enough to make me see stars. I guess I could forgive the second one with enough time.

"Well look who it is," I said and came to my full height.

She looked up at me but wasn't intimidated. She didn't look mad or sad. In fact, she had no expression at all.

"Yeah. Look who it is. You guys looking for a shower and chow? Because you need it."

Roz crossed her arms and stared at Sails. Sails met her gaze and didn't flinch.

I leaned over and whispered in Joel's ear, "Girl fight, bro."

He pushed me off.

"You seen Lee?" I asked Sails.

"No. If you want to thank him I'll pass along your message. Do yourself a favor and let it go. It sucks, but it was for the best," she said and moved away.

Joel got in her face.

"It was for the best? He was just a kid. What if it was your kid, huh?"

"It was my kids, but now they're gone. If you'll excuse me," she said and moved away.

Shit.

Joel looked like he wanted to say something but he didn't. Anna glanced between us and didn't say a word before moving off into the crowd.

The base of operations was made up of a hospital and a bunch of smaller buildings. People scurried around, most of them armed. I hadn't seen so many people in one place in a long time and it was comforting.

Hand painted signs hung on hastily constructed signposts indicating in which way lay food and supplies. I spotted one in particular and almost broke into tears.

'Showers.'

I smacked Joel and pointed. He nodded but couldn't seem to take his eyes off the departing figure of Anna Sails.

"You like that?"

"I'm not happy, bro."

"Join the fucking club."

I pointed at a sign that read "food" and we moved toward it.

"Chow first. Then I'm going to shower so long I turn into a giant prune."

"Squids and water," Joel said and then led the way.

They fed us in an overcrowded mess hall filled with a mix of military, military wannabes, and civvies. There were lines drawn, like a prison mess hall. A group of survivalist types complete with "been in the mountains for months" beards sat near a couple of families but the groups didn't look at each other. The military men and women strutted around with weapons on open display.

"Pass the salt?" a man asked me.

He sat with four kids and a wife who hovered over the little ones while they ate dry cereal and stared around the room with wide eyes.

The kitchen had canned supplies and boxes containing even more boxes of crackers. There were five-gallon jugs of bug juice and sliders that tasted like slimy vegetarian fake meat. I don't know where they got the stuff but my stomach thanked me. My guts weren't so happy an hour later but I rode it out and then came back and begged for more. I'm not a little guy and it takes a lot to feed this zombie killing machine.

The rest of the partially formed base was obviously in transition when we arrived. A steady stream of cars and trucks roared into and out of the base. There was a constant unholy racket of helicopters thumping at the sky as they roared in and then back out. Most delivered supplies but a lot of them carried away people. Folks that were dressed in civvies and carried bags or stuffed suit cases. Where was everyone headed? If it was somewhere safe I wanted to go there now.

Like the empty field we'd flown over yesterday this place had tents everywhere. They told us to go to some section that me nor Joel Kelly could make heads or tails of. Might as well have been some Sudoku puzzle for all the sense it made.

I wasn't complaining. I can't say how relieved I am that I'm somewhere surrounded by guns and people who know how to use them. The food might not be the best but it was food. I've been so hungry over the last ten days I'm sure I've lost about fifteen pounds.

We ate and tried to talk but we didn't get a lot of answers. I turned to the guy that had asked for the salt and asked him what was happening in the world. How far had the virus spread? Were all of the other states affected?

"When the televisions and radio stations died we lost touch with the outside world and just waited. We ran out of food a few days ago and started moving around. A convoy found us and rescued me and the family. Thank god for the military."

"So you don't know what's going on in the rest of the world?" I had so many questions but everyone I talked to had a similar answer. Even the military guys didn't know what was going on.

One thing I learned was that there'd been mass desertion, as the enlisted grew worried about families and just left their posts and stations.

"All I know is I got food and water and a warm place for my family. That's good enough for me." He turned away.

I resisted the urge to grab him by the shirt collar and demand answers. Instead I snapped my plastic fork in half. I probably just needed to go find a place to curl up and sleep for the rest of the day. First we needed to spend some time trying to clean off two weeks of blood and filth.

The tent was huge and sectioned off for men and women.

It wasn't warm and the soap were cakes of white with other people's hair in them. I didn't care, and judging by the sounds of others near me (including Roz, who hummed a song in a bad falsetto) no one else did either.

Not much of a shower, but I was left grinning and shivering. Piles of clothing, most of it military, were in a corner. I pawed through it until I found something big enough to fit me. Must have been someone's shitty idea of a joke because the only pants my size were a pair of old dungarees that were loose in the waist and too short by a few inches, but they were better than my beat to hell overalls. The shirt was digital camo and had enough arm pockets to hold a few odds and ends. I filled one with .45 ammo and another with 9mm.

I strapped my trusty .45 around my waist, then grabbed a huge pea coat and fell into it. Warmth eventually set in while we stood around talking about the wonders of running water. Christy looked dour and when Roz suggested looking for a bed we followed.

"Sleep. I need a week of it," I said.

"Me too, man. I'm as tired as I've been in my whole damn life. Even boot wasn't this much work."

Together we went to find a couple of cots.

10:30 hours approximate
Location: San Diego, CA - US Naval Hospital

Roz and Christy found a cot and a sleeping bag right next to each other; no one else had claimed them, so they settled in. Joel and I nodded at Roz and moved on to find a corner of our own.

I settled back on the cot and stared at the ceiling. Someone had left a pile of magazines in a corner but who cared about that shit anymore? Damn world was gone and I was supposed to read celebrity gossip? Hell, most of those chumps were dead anyway if Los Angeles went down like San Diego.

The enclosure was huge and filled with sorry sorts. We walked up and down aisles before deciding that if someone came for this pair of cots they'd have to be bigger and meaner to make us move.

People moved in and out of the area. Kids cried. Babies howled. Mothers shushed, and fathers looked dour.

"When do we tell them we're enlisted?" I asked Joel quietly.

Joel leaned over close and whispered. "I don't know if we should. Something weird about this base."

I had to agree with Joel's assessment. Since we'd arrived no one had answered our questions. They told us there'd be time for that later. We should settle in, relax and eat. No one would come clean about what was going on.

I'd tried to ask a few people, but they were all tightlipped. Then I found a guy named Edward Bowls. He was in his mid-fifties and coughed all the time. One time I thought I saw his hand come away with blood but he covered it up.

"It's bad out there," he'd said when no one else was around. "They try to make it seem like this is isolated but it's not. The states are falling fast and there doesn't seem to be anyway to stop the spread of the virus. It doesn't get everyone but it gets most. Some have managed to setup battle lines and quarantine zones. I heard that Montana is pretty clear but there ain't shit in that state to begin with, just a bunch of open space. Plus everyone's got guns."

"So not everywhere is as bad as San Diego."

"Yeah but some places are worse. I heard Lee was up north and is heading back up there. Lee's in charge I guess, cept he ain't military." Edward leaned over and coughed until he was out of breath.

"He's not? He sure seems like it." I tried to play it cool.

"Some group of mercenaries. That's what I heard. I guess he was over in Afghanistan spreading freedom with a machine gun before his boys got called back home."

"Mercenaries." Joel swore.

"That bad?" I asked but neither one answered.

"I heard stuff and it wasn't pretty," Joel said and put his arm over his eyes.

I lay back on the hard cot and tried not to think. That lasted for about fifteen seconds.

"So mercenaries, like Black Water. US has been using them for years, right?"

"I guess, man. I never ran into them when I was over there."

What if Lee had been right? What if monkeys flew out of my ass? One thing I'd learned in this new world was to stop dwelling on the what-if's. All those got you was a big cup of regret and not much else.

But questions swirled around my head. Craig was fine all day and the night before. What was different about the disease when it attacked him? Why was it delayed?

Then it hit me. He'd gone back to Roz's house and secured some of our gear. What if one of the things had gotten at him and he kept that part of her trip quiet?

Shit.

"Are you sure you didn't you see any sign of the virus in Craig?" I asked Joel.

"You've asked me that a hundred times. I don't know, man, I was there too and I don't know."

"Right? I know he was fine. I know it. Lee had no right to do what he did."

"Lee's probably gone now, so what are you gonna do?" Joel asked me.

"Go after him? Wait for him to get back. I don't care. I just want a chance at his ass."

"He seems to be in charge or something. Weird that he doesn't wear any insignia but everyone knows who he is."

"He's an asshole," I said.

"Truer words, brother."

Joel rolled over and covered his head with his pillow.

Asshole.

# # #

We woke to screams.

I sat up in semi-darkness and felt around for my side arm. It was under my pillow, that's right. Tucked next to a backup mag. Joel was on his feet and checking over his own weapon. We weren't the only ones. There were so many armed folks you'd think we were at an NRA sleep over.

A guy dressed in fatigues ripped the tent entrance open and shouted over the rows of cots.

"Up. Everyone up. Move quickly to the landing pad. Choppers are arriving. When you get the sign, you keep low and get on board. Got it? You don't listen and you get left behind."

I shook my head and rubbed my eyes. My head felt like it was full of cotton and my eyes were gummed shut. Joel was already strapping on his gear and appeared to have been up for hours. I wished I had a double dose of energy drink, then a bottle of whiskey to wash that shit back with. Thai whiskey. I'd crush a few heads for some.

The civilians around us rose and packed quickly. Kids were quieted and shuffled out. It didn't turn into a panic until the guns started to boom outside.

I pushed through the throng with Joel Kelly close behind. Roz was on her feet with a backpack over her shoulder. She tugged out a handgun and held it at her side.

Christy stuck to her side but she was clenching her fists open and shut over and over again. I dropped my pack to the ground and opened it. Moving things around, I found what I was looking for.

"Don't shoot anyone. You know how these work, right?"

It was the little Sig Sauer 229 I'd found on Monster Ken an eternity ago.

Christy took the gun and looked it over. She racked the slide back to inspect the chamber and then let it slam shut.

"I've played a lot of video games."

"Good," I said. "Now don't shoot anyone unless they're a threat."

"Yep."

She lifted her head and nodded at me. Confidence, though a spark at best, showed.

"What now?" Roz yelled over the noise.

I tried to smile at Roz but it came out as a sneer. She thumped me in the chest, then kissed her fingers and smacked me across the cheek, not too hard, kind of a love tap. Then she did the same to Joel Kelly.

"Let's go kick some ass," Kelly said.

"Or haul ass," I said.

Together we navigated the throng and moved to the entrance.

Our quarters weren't even two hundred feet from the entrance to the base so we got a quick appraisal of the action and it wasn't good. Not good at all.

Joel must not have believed his eyes because he moved toward the gate. The wrong way. Stupid jarhead.

Civilians streamed past us in a panic, clutching children close. A man lugged a huge suitcase a few feet then looked over his shoulder and gasped. He tossed the bag to the side of the pathway and started to push through the crowd.

Men and women, some in white gowns and others in wheel chairs spewed out of the hospital doors. Other's watched from windows with huge eyes.

I watched too. I watched and I got scared.

As far as the eye could see they came. The mass was the largest I'd seen yet, even surpassing the horde that we'd spotted moving through the city. They stumbled toward the fence in their greed for human flesh.

It wasn't an easy task to navigate the traps and bodies left to rot from the previous incursion, but they came at us anyway. They poured over the remains of the crashed chopper we'd arrived in. They came even though gunfire smashed into them from a running squad making their way for the gate.

An enemy with any sense would have ducked and moved as they sought to find firing positions. These had no care in the world for tactics. These monsters just wanted to eat.

The dead numbered in the thousands, or maybe even the tens of thousands.

Guns opened up in force this time. They fired without respite, .50 cals along the outside walls and men positioned over the newly constructed mesh gate. If we thought we were safe, it was an illusion. As soon as they hit the chain link, our safety, that illusion was gone.

Joel dashed to the line and tapped a gunner on the shoulder. The other man didn't look at him, just kept on shooting. Joel pulled his pistol, took careful aim, and fired.

Joel was like that. If there was a fight he was there. I wasn't like that. I would fight if I had too but this was too much. The men and women defending us were looking at a painful death.

If I left now I could probably slip into the mass of people and use my size to my advantage to fight my way to the front of the line. If there was a truck or chopper headed away from this mess, I wanted to be on it.

Who was Joel Kelly anyway? Just a guy I'd been stuck with since our boat was overrun. We'd put up with each other for days. We'd argued, fought together, and even come to be friends. I'd saved his life and he'd saved mine.

"Take the kid and go," I said to Roz. "Just go. I'll be there soon."

"Fuck you, sailor boy. I'm getting in this war."

Christy grinned up at her. Who the hell was I to tell them to run away?

Jesus Christ, was I the only sane one? Now was my chance. I hadn't asked to be shackled with this bunch. I might be better off on my own.

Who was I kidding?

"Oh, fuck a duck!" I said and went to join Joel.

I wasn't the only one. A number of civilians did the dumb thing, like me, and moved toward the action. They carried what weapons they could gather, mostly melee, but some had guns. Military guys roared up in jeeps and spun to expose beds laden with huge cases. These were dragged into the center of the action and broken open. Automatic weapons gleamed back at us. Cases of ammo and magazines, some full, were also left out for us.

I grabbed a machine gun of some sort, probably some gun Joel could wax poetically about for days telling me the exact length of the trigger action and round capacity. In another box I found full magazines. I picked up a box of shells and went to find a nice corner to plan my death.

The horde came on and was answered with lead. As the horde closed, and even picked up speed, it became apparent that we had minutes at most. You'd think that twenty or thirty people shooting could handle anything but we were outnumbered. For every body that fell there were five to take its place.

And there were shufflers. A lot of shufflers. They were in the pack but many of them held back as the slow ones went to do their dirty work. I swear those goddamn things still have half a brain.

The fortifications outside of the gate did a lot to help slow the dead. They got hung up on barbed wire and stuck to posts. Some were fired upon while others left to lift their hands and reach for us in vain. Losers.

I ducked and moved toward Joel Kelly. He was outside the gate, on one knee, aiming and firing with grim determination. His position was right next to an overturned truck. I touched his shoulder and he looked back and shot me a wink.

"Glad you could make it, bud." He aimed and dropped a woman dressed in the remains of a nightgown. She fell without a sound and was quickly trampled beneath the mass behind her.

Next to him was someone I didn't expect. Anna Sails fired in rapid succession with a gun as long as her legs, and she wielded it like a pro. She fired, shifted, aimed, fired again, and every time her gun boomed one of them dropped.

"Civilians are being moved out in trucks. Buy them time. Fall back when the horde gets close. We got a surprise for them." A man with a bullhorn shouted at us. I thought it might be Lee and had a hastily constructed plan where he accidentally takes a bullet, but when I looked back it wasn't him.

It didn't take long for us to create a wall of bodies but it didn't do much to deter them. A couple of shufflers leapt off the top and came down near some of our guys. They were quickly shot down, but it was close.

The first line must have gotten some signal. They dropped down low while the line behind them stopped firing. They scurried back and the second line opened up again. We were about fifteen feet from the gate and when they called for us to do the same.

Five or six guys ran out as we retreated. They carried bandoliers covered in metal globes. They stopped, pulled pins, and tossed a wave of grenades at the approaching horde. I was already on the run when the explosions shook the ground and I didn't look back.

We were cutting it close. The dead were only a few feet away when Anna Sails stowed her weapon on her shoulder and ran after us. I kept an eye on her and even shot a shuffler as it leapt out of the mass. I hit him with three or four bullets but they only ripped into his body. He was blown to the side, but he was a quick one and rolled to his feet. With an Olympian leap he managed to take down one of our guys. The soldier howled in fury but got off a shot and hit the bastard in the head. Brains exploded and one of his buddies stopped to pull him out from under the corpse.

"Everyone in, now!" The guy with the bullhorn roared, so we hauled ass.

As we cleared the gate the heavy machinery we'd seen earlier in the day roared to life. A pair of fences sections had been tied to the bulldozer. It rammed into the horde with a sound that will haunt my nightmares for years to come. It came to a halt after crushing a great many of them, and then backed up with a flash of yellow lights and piercing alarm.

Joel helped Anna in but she shrugged off his hand and went to stand with a group she seemed to know. They set up a new firing line behind the fence while the rest of our guys filed inside. It was all high fives and way to go's but not everyone was happy. Edward, the man I'd met in the mess hall, looked haunted. He also looked like he needed to find a bucket.

Behind us, civilians moved onto trucks that lurched away. Some didn't wait and tried to crowd on to full trucks or jump on board before they had stopped moving. When the Z's hit the fence it was pandemonium.

"We should go, Joel," I said and grabbed his arm.

He pointed toward the crane we'd seen when we first arrived.

Its arm moved into the air, lifting a huge claw and then it swept own and cleared a path. Not even a hundred Z's could stand up to the crane's power as it swept back and forth.

The mass was here, though, and it was a matter of time before this entire base was overrun.

A shuffler hit the fence and tried to climb it, but Anna Sails shot him through the head.

"Yeah, it's time," Joel said.

I looked around and spotted Roz and Christy. She'd abandoned the little handgun in favor of a machine gun. It has huge in her hands as she moved away.

Our pace was brisk and soon we ran into others that were fleeing. We had to slow, but at least we were moving toward safety.

Then I heard a sound to my left. The horde had swung around or broken off and had reached the fenced in there. Reinforced by long metal bars the chain-link still wasn't strong enough to withstand the impact. A pair of shufflers launched themselves at the top of the wall and one managed to reach the razor wire. He got hung up. I took a lot of joy in pausing for a minute to shoot it three or four times. No headshot but he slumped after the last bullet ripped through his upper body.

"The fence isn't going to hold. Move!" A soldier said and then broke into a run.

The crane swung its arm back and forth but the driver must have seen the futility of his action and decided it was time to make his getaway. The crane backed up and all those tons of metal began a slow crawl through the dead. None rose from where it passed.

"Come on, you big idiot." Roz grabbed my arm and pulled.

I joined our motley group of five even though I was sure we were about to be over run. Thousands of them behind, and thousands to on our flank. We weren't going to last much longer unless we found a transport.

A pair of HUMVEEs pulled into the street to my right and then opened up with machine guns. The guys on the guns swept back and forth as they shredded the front ranks.

A rending crash behind. I didn't have to look around to know that the fence was gone.

We ran with me in the lead because I was the biggest. We hit the mass of other survivors looking for a way out and I wasn't shy about pushing through them.

The line of trucks and cars took on as many as they could. It was a full blown panic as people fought to get on anything that moved. Women and children were pushed aside. Anger boiled but this was no time to crack some heads and teach manners.

Some ran. They just bolted in every direction, barreling into anyone blocking their way.

Explosions behind. I looked over my shoulder and found a group of soldiers tossing more grenades at the mass of Z's. Bodies and parts of bodies flew.

We were brought to a halt by a couple of guys trying to sort the evacuees.

"Civilians that way." One of them pointed at a scrambling mass.

A second line fed to huge military transports that was at least somewhat organized. Men and women in uniform jumped onto transports, some as they roared off.

"We're enlisted, man."

"Right. Move your ass or we'll drop you right where you stand."

A couple of people picked that minute to try and break through the line and run toward the military trucks. They were met with the butt of rifles. Another civilian got wind of the action and screamed.

"They aren't letting us out!"

Joel and I exchanged glances just before the first shot rang.

A civilian in ragged jeans and a white t-shirt covered in holes pulled a pistol and pointed it at one of the guys in green. He pointed back and shouting broke out. The guard looked at us and lowered his gun as well.

"It's cool, man. We'll just find another ride," Joel said.

Didn't these guys have a secret military code or something? Joel was dressed in the remains of his combat gear and if there was a man with more military bearing, he wasn't here.

I backed up a step, taking Roz with me. Then a figure pushed between us.

"Lower that gun, soldier," she said.

Anna Sails to the rescue.

"They can't join us, ma'am," he replied.

"These guys are with me and they're enlisted. Just make a hole," she said and pushed forward.

The two looked at us in confusion. Then it evaporated as shots broke out near us.

"Oh, fuck this shit," Joel said and grabbed Roz's hand.

The two sides got tired of shouting at each other and someone fired. I couldn't tell which let the first bullet fly but it was a massacre after that.

I backed up and then grabbed Christy's hand and tugged her after Joel.

Anna Sails followed and together we ran back toward the horde.

#

Chaos behind. Chaos to the sides.

It was either risk a bullet or run.

We ran.

The fence on the east side of the little base went down. I fired a few rounds as we ran but it was like trying to stop a wave with a BB gun.

Shots continued to ring out as we hauled ass. The pair of HUMVEEs we'd seen earlier backed up as they fired. I smacked Joel's arm to get his attention. He veered toward the transports.

Joel waved his hands to stop the trucks. They slowed as they fired.

I turned and shot a Z in the neck as it came at us. There was another behind him and when I fired a burst, the bolt slapped open with a clang as I ran dry. I reached for a mag, but realized too late that I was totally out.

Fuck that. I swung the gun around, burned the shit out of my hands on the barrel, ignored it to turn the gun into a bat, and hit the Z so hard it did a mid-air summersault and landed in a splatter of crushed head and leaking brain matter.

Five or six more were right behind.

"Nice shot," Anna said beside me. She turned to her side, raised a huge hand gun and fired. Seriously, it was like something Dirty Harry would carry.

A shuffler leapt out of the mass and was on Sails before I could fire. They tumbled to the ground and the bastard went at her. Sails was good, fast; she got her gun in the way and smacked the Shuffler across the mouth. He howled and dove in for her neck.

I grabbed him by the back of his ratty-ass clothes, and lifted him straight off the ground making my ankle want to screech in pain. He was covered in open sores and bled some kind of mucus from multiple wounds but I didn't give a shit.

Sails might be a pain in the ass but none of us were going down under a shuffler. I'd put a bullet in her skull first.

She pulled herself across the ground, looked up, and blew the head off one of the dead that was headed straight for me.

The shuffler fought like a man with twice his strength. He got me good across the gut and most of the air left my lungs. Then his elbow connected with my head and I saw stars.

I lifted him above my head with both arms and then flung him down on the back of the HUMVEE so hard his head split like a fucking melon. Sails had to pull me away from kicking his twice-dead ass.

"I'm Marine Sergeant Joel Kelly. Got room for us?" Joel stood near the front of the transport.

"Pretty fucking full, Sarge. We got…" I couldn't hear the rest because the machine gunner blasted a line of lead across the approaching dead.

There were so many of them that we didn't stand a chance. The walls were down and we were being overrun.

Joel grabbed Roz and Christy and stuffed them into the back of the Humvee. I scooped up Sails and dragged her to the other side of the truck and banged on the door. It opened and the face of a young soldier poked out.

Anna was having difficulty breathing and gasped when I picked her up.

"I'm staying with you guys," Sails said.

I ignored her.

"Put her on your lap. You're welcome," I said and pushed her toward the door.

"Idiot! I don't need saving! Just let me stand and fight with you guys."

"Get in or I'll put you in," I said as I towered over her.

The machine gunner opened up again and dropped at least a half dozen.

"I'm staying!" She pushed against my damaged chest.

"Anna, please. Get in. We're all getting out of here," I said.

She looked me up and down and then nodded and crawled in.

"Better than being tossed to the dead," I said. Thoughts of Anna backing up Lee made me second-guess my actions. Maybe I should have tossed her to the horde.

The back was stuffed and there was no way for me and Joel to squeeze in. Joel winked at me through the opening and then slammed the door shut. He came around the side of the transport firing.

I closed the door and joined him.

"Hold on, gents!" The machine gunner roared and pointed at the back of the HUMVEE.

A whole world of hurt ran at us. The dead were here and we were screwed.

Joel was the first to make the leap. He got on the back of the transport and shimmied up the angled back until the gunner helped him. Then he hung onto the plates on the side of the gun.

The HUMVEE lurched into motion with me standing in the middle of the zombie fucking apocalypse holding my dick.

"Wait for me!" I yelled and leapt.

I missed.

The first Z came at me so I clothes-lined the asshole. A shot and something buzzed past my neck. I looked over my shoulder and there was Joel Kelly, holding onto the back of a giant machine gun while he somehow pulled his side arm and shot a dead fuck through the head.

This guy should be in a video game.

I hauled ass, jumped for the back and started to slide back off. Joel dropped his gun, grabbed the machine gun mount with both hands and stuck his boot right next to my face. I grabbed hold and tried to haul myself up but a Z got my leg.

I kicked back a few times and got him in the face. Bone crunched as his nose was crushed but I didn't have time to gloat because the truck lurched into motion and I had to hold onto Joel Kelly's leg for dear life.

I crawled up the back of the HUMVEE until I was able to reach the gunner. Him and Joel reached out and pulled me the rest of the way then I was clutching the back of the gun mount.

"Haul ass!" The gunner pounded the top of the truck.

We broke across a parking lot, ran over a tent, hit the side of the building and that almost knocked me clear but I had a death grip.

Then we were past the little base and behind the line of trucks.

"Next stop, L A." The gunner grinned.

"Great. I need some new underwear," I said over the roaring wind.

The gunner smiled again and patted my shoulder. He ducked back into the vehicle for a minute.

"Joel, man. I owe you."

"Yeah you do. Dumb squid."

"Words hurt," I said. "Especially from a dumb jarhead."

"Don't get all mushy on me. Christ. I've had enough of this day and if you start bawling I'm going to have the gunner shoot me in the fucking head."

"Okay man, I won't, but I want to tell you something."

"I ain't marrying you."

"Thank the fuck Christ." We hit a bump and I came down on my sore chest again. After an epic swearing session I got my breath back.

"Gonna make it?"

"As long as you got my back I think I'll be okay. You're like a brother, Joel. Nah. You are my brother." I said it and meant it. We'd seen a lot of shit over the last few weeks but one thing hadn't changed. One thing had been there to help me survive and cope with this new world and that was Marine Sergeant Joel "Cruze" Kelly.

"Know something?" Joel asked.

We bounced up the road, slowed at a cross street, and then maneuvered around a wreck.

"Huh?" I asked, expecting some kind of brotherhood of war speech.

"I'm glad we're moving. I just farted and it's a reeker. Sorry about that." He looked at me with a smirk. "Brother."

I couldn't help it. I laughed until tears streamed down my face.

"Can you guys drive faster? Something died back here!" I roared at the driver.

"Sure, man." The driver called back.

"I can't hang on that long."

"Hitchhikers take what they can get." He laughed from inside.

"I hope he's kidding." I said to the gunner.

He didn't answer, just looked up.

Overhead, a helicopter roared away from the base and headed north. If Lee was on it I wished him well, because when I found him again he'd answer questions with my size fourteen boot up his ass.

This is Machinist Mate First Class Jackson Creed and I am still alive.

THE END

The sequel will arrive in early 2014

Z-RISEN: OUTCASTS

Read a sample of book two at:

HTTP://Z-RISEN.COM

Read the book set in the same universe as Z-Risen:

BEYOND THE BARRIERS

BEYOND THE BARRIERS is a military style zombie book set in the same world as Z-Risen.

When the dead rise, Ex-Special Forces soldier Erik Tragger flees to the mountains to wait out the end of the world. Cut off from civilization for months, he returns to find cities ruined and ruled by the walking dead.

Tragger reluctantly joins a group of survivors with a plan: flee to Portland where humanity is carving out a stronghold. But along the way they face opposition at every turn—the dead, rogue military forces, looters... and a new enemy more dangerous than any they have yet encountered.

Among the stumbling, mindless zombies walk the ghouls. The ghouls are living dead creatures that not only strategize and plan, but also possess the ability to guide their shambling brothers.

With weapons and supplies dwindling, Erik and his companions will faceoff against millions of the dead who have but one goal: complete eradication of the last of the living.

About the Author

Timothy W. Long has been writing tales and stories since he could hold a crayon and has also read enough books to choke a landfill. He has a fascination with all things zombies, a predilection for hula-girl dolls, and a deep-seated need to jot words on paper and thrust them at people.

Tim swears that if he is ever stuck on a deserted island with a zombie, no matter how attractive, he will bash in her brains.
Really!

HTTP://TIMOTHYWLONG.COM

HTTP://WWW.FACEBOOK.COM/TIMOTHYWLONG

@TIMWLONG

Made in the USA
Lexington, KY
08 March 2014